REINED IN

VICKI THARP

JPC PUBLISHING

REINED IN

Reined In is a work of fiction. Names, characters, places and incidents either are the product of the author's imagination or are used fictitiously, and any resemblance to actual persons, living or dead, business establishments, events, or locals, is entirely coincidental.

Original Cover Design by Rebecca Pau at the Final Wrap

ISBN 978-1-948798-07-5

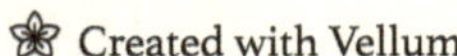 Created with Vellum

1

———

1976. A new year. A new rodeo season. Time for hard work to pay off.

Thursday night found Levi Banks at the Travis County Fairgrounds on the outskirts of Austin, Texas. He backed up his chestnut quarter horse, Chunk, into the back of the box at the end of the arena, preparing for his final practice run of the day. Bob Forney, one of the men from No Bull Roughstock Supply, loaded another steer into the chute, as Chunk danced beneath Levi, eager to run.

Levi's hazer, Cooter Craw, was the best a bulldogger could ask for. As a friend, he was even better. Cooter nodded from the box on the other side of the steer, indicating he was ready. In turn, Levi nodded to Forney.

As the calf burst from the chute, Levi noticed movement out of the corner of his eye. Olivia Marsh. His heart stumbled a beat, and Cooter took off, catching Levi off guard. A split second behind, he put his heels to Chunk's sides. His horse scrambled out of the box, galloping after the steer.

On his best black and white Pinto, Cooter rode hard to keep the steer running straight, but with Levi and Chunk playing catch-up, the calf veered too far to the left. If Levi had been smart, he'd have pulled Chunk up short. Diving off a galloping horse onto an animal with horns was dangerous enough without pushing a bad situation.

But this was the last practice he'd get before the first rodeo of the spring series kicked off the next day.

At least that was the excuse he went with instead of blaming his actions on ego, and a stupid, childish need of his to show off to the woman who'd made it abundantly clear that she wouldn't spare the energy to piss on him if he struck a match and lit himself on fire.

He pressed Chunk faster. Leaning out of the saddle, he dropped into the hole, his arm across the steer, his right foot still in the stirrup. At the point of no return, Chunk surged a little too hard, a little too fast, cutting off the steer. The steer skidded to a stop.

Levi cussed, his body landing too far forward to wrap his hands around the horns. His boots slid through the deep arena dirt, the steer's horn catching his shirt and raking across his ribs. Levi hissed, sucking up the pain.

Tumbling to the ground, he managed to tuck and roll, jamming his shoulder hard enough to bruise, but not hard enough to dislocate.

He grunted as he lay flat on his back in the dirt. He chanced a glance at Olivia. She had a supercilious grin on her face as she turned and walked away. Cooter rounded up the steer as Chunk ambled over and nibbled at the tear in Levi's shirt. The gelding pulled on the ripped cotton, tearing the hole even wider.

"Thanks, asshole." Levi scrunched his fingers through Chunk's forelock and gave him a pat on the flat of his jaw.

Slowly, Levi rolled to his hands and knees and stood, dirt raining down.

Cooter and his horse trotted over. "If you were tryin' to impress the ladies, I think ya missed your mark."

Levi retrieved his hat and knocked off the dirt. "I'm not trying to impress nobody."

"Good thing."

Levi chuckled and he felt it in his stiffening shoulder. "You're an asshole, too." He gathered up his reins and led Chunk out of the arena.

Cooter laughed and dismounted, catching up with Levi. Together they returned to the barn. Levi wanted to give Chunk a good brush out and a bath now that it had warmed up.

"I'd sure like to know what ya did to piss that Marsh woman off," Cooter said, his West Texas drawl as thick as it had always been. He spat a wad of tobacco, aiming for the scurrying dung beetle. "Usually she's right even-tempered for a woman."

"Best not let her hear you say that. You think she's mad now?" Levi stopped at his stall and started untacking Chunk. "For your information, I didn't do anything. She's probably mad because she still hasn't found someone she trusts to manage her stock on the road."

Cooter looked at Levi thoughtfully and spat again for good measure. The old man scratched at the gray-grizzled stubble along his sun-weathered jaw. "Naw," Cooter said at last. "Ain't that. She's got her back up and her claws out like a woman scorned. Trust me. I've seen enough of 'em in my time. I'd rather wrestle a rabid wolf than tangle with one of them."

Well, damn. That didn't bode well. "That may be, Coot, but for some reason, she's latched onto me as her designated whipping boy."

Cooter got a knowing, sly glimmer in his old, rheumy eyes. "That's the kind of woman you want to tame and take to bed. If you're man enough."

That the old man directly contradicted himself wasn't lost on

Levi. He threw his head back and laughed. "That kind of woman chews you up and spits you out. There's no taming that woman even if I wanted. Which I don't."

It was Cooter's turn to laugh. He collected his paint horse. As he walked away, he said, "You keep telling yourself that."

Levi didn't have to. He'd learned a hard lesson after breaking things off with Patty Bennett. That lesson? He still hadn't gotten over Cora Hayes. Probably never would. How could he love another woman when his heart was still broken?

———

Once again, the rodeo crowd had taken over a local bar for the weekend, outnumbering the locals by three to one. In a dark corner of the Rough Rider, a country bar like any other, Olivia nursed a cheap, warm bottle of beer that tasted like watered down piss. She glanced around. Neon beer signs, jukebox, a scrap of wood on the ground people called a dance floor. Tight jeans and low-cut shirts. People laughing. People crying in their beer.

A local boy who had been eying her for the past thirty minutes must have consumed enough liquid courage because he stood, hitched up his jeans, and sauntered her way. Literally, sauntered. He'd watched one too many John Wayne movies.

"Ma'am." He tipped his jet-black cowboy hat. Everyone wanted to be the bad cowboy.

Olivia leaned back and finished the last of her beer. "Can I help you?"

The man got a grin on his face, and if Olivia squinted a bit, she might be able to call him cute. She squinted. Okay, maybe not.

He pointed to her beer. "Can I buy you another?"

"Thanks, but I was about to leave." Olivia weighed the

cheap price of a beer to the heavy toll of making idle chitchat while almost too exhausted to lift the bottle, much less flirt, dance, or have sex. Other women might gladly take him up on his offer.

"It's early yet, beautiful." The man confidently fed her the line as if the compliment had worked many times before. He pulled out a chair and went to sit down when a meaty hand clamped down on his shoulder. The man stilled and glanced over his shoulder at Levi Banks.

Great. She'd take the John Wayne wanna-be over Banks. The piece of shit.

"Beat it, buddy," Levi said.

When a man wrestled six-hundred-pound animals for a living, people tended not to mess with them.

The man looked like he'd quickly calculated his options and chose the one that meant life. "She your girl or something?" He must have needed that final confirmation.

"Something like that," Levi said.

Olivia decided an unknown beat the devil she already knew. "Hardly."

One final cutting look from Levi and the wanna-be left.

Levi held two frosty mugs of dark draft in his hand. He placed one in front of her and sat.

She accepted the beer, because, hey, good, cold beer shouldn't go to waste. "What are you doing?"

With half a smile he said, "What's it look like I'm doing?"

Olivia didn't have to squint or drink a gallon of beer to appreciate the way Levi filled out a pair of Wranglers or the way his crooked smile added to his so-called charm. She could see why her cousin had fallen for him not too long out of high school. Good thing Olivia knew the truth about him or she might be sorely tempted to take him to her bed for a quick tumble or two.

"I'm not going to sleep with you." Maybe if she said it out loud, both he and her subconscious would get the message.

Levi grinned—full on—and Olivia's heart betrayed her and kicked at her sternum like a damn mule. He took a long drag on his beer, and she couldn't take her eyes off the play of his throat. His grin got impossibly wider when he caught her staring. "Don't flatter yourself, boss lady."

Boss lady. That got Olivia's back up, and her laugh came out bitter around the burned edges. "You're telling me that if I invited you back to my motel room, you'd say no?" Olivia expected him to disagree, after all, the rodeo had no shortage of randy cowboys.

His cocky smile fell away. "What do you have against me anyway?"

"You're an asshole."

"You don't even know me."

"I know enough."

In Olivia's opinion, any man who didn't want to have anything to do with his own kid, especially one as cute as Clementine, wasn't the kind of man Olivia needed in her life, even if he could scratch an itch. She held his gaze as Levi eyed her over the top of his beer.

"How? How do you 'know enough?'"

"Does it matter?"

"Does to me."

She hadn't expected he'd be man enough to admit that.

"Until you took over for Scottie Hines, I've never even talked to you, yet you hated me from the outset."

"Hate is a very strong word."

His expression never changed, but the tick of muscle beneath one eye said she was trampling his patience. "*Strongly disliked.*"

Someone turned the jukebox up. Olivia had to lean forward

and practically shout when she said, "You used to date my cousin."

"Who?" Levi hollered back.

"Mae," Olivia said. "Mae Jordan."

Levi's mouth went flat, and he might have muttered a curse, but not loud enough to be heard over the jukebox and the general hubbub of the crowd. "Nice girl, but you gotta know that if her lips are moving, she's lying, right?"

Yep. Certifiable, grade A asshole. "Is that any way to talk about—" Olivia cut herself off. She wouldn't get anywhere going *there* with him. Lord knew Mae never had.

"Talk about what?"

"Never mind."

Levi leaned back and took another drag from his beer. "How is old Mae these days?"

Olivia choked and spit out her beer. "Dead."

———

Friday night at the rodeo had always been Levi's favorite. Even more so than Sunday night when the checks were on the line. Fridays were a time of hope and anticipation for the weekend to come. Even the energy of the crowd differed. And even after his years of junior, amateur, and professional rodeo, Levi still got a slight twist in his gut in the time leading up to his run.

That knot of tension didn't worry him. The tension told him that what he did for a living still mattered.

In the barn aisle, Levi adjusted the pad beneath Chunk's saddle and tightened the girth. A few aisles over, Cora's larger-than-life laugh blasted through the general noise of the competitors getting ready for their events. Horses whinnied, and

Smokey Dunn's pissy mare kicked at her stall, the *bang, bang, bang*, echoing throughout the barn.

Cooter came by and leaned an arm across Chunk's withers. "Ya doing okay?"

Levi took the tail of his latigo and tucked it into the keeper on his saddle. "The usual Friday night jitters. I'll be —"

"That's not what I'm talking about, and ya know it, son." With a finger, Cooter nudged up the brim of his sweat and dirt-smudged cowboy hat.

Levi should have never told Cooter about Mae's death, but the old man had known her in those early days before Levi had gone pro. As such, he felt he'd owed the old man the courtesy of the notification.

Way back then, Cooter had been the only one he'd shown the engagement ring he'd bought for Mae before their relationship had tanked. His friend had been privy to how hard it had been for Levi to break it off in the end, and he'd witnessed Mae's pre-breakup downward spiral turn into an ugly, gut-wrenching nosedive.

One she hadn't been able to pull out of.

Apparently, in Mae's case, rock-bottom meant six feet under.

"It's almost been a year since she died."

"Yeah, and ya found out about her dying last night. It's okay to let yourself grieve. Deep down, Mae was a good girl."

"A troubled girl. I couldn't love her enough —" Levi's throat got tight and his voice caught, even after so much time. Even after he'd discovered what true love was. *Fuck.* "Maybe if I'd—"

"No, son. Don't be letting your mind go there. That ain't your burden to bear. If you'da hung on any tighter, she'd have sunk you just as surely as that hunk of ice sunk the Titanic."

"If things had been different, if she had accepted the help, maybe then—"

"You can't force people to change. They gotta want it for themselves."

Levi pinched the bridge of his nose and rubbed at his eyes with his thumb and forefinger. Cooter was right. Didn't make accepting the truth any easier.

Cooter patted Chunk on his muscular neck and stepped back. "Time to get your head on straight. Those steers ain't gonna wrestle themselves."

Clearing his throat, Levi said, "Yeah, sure."

Because he had time to spare, Levi warmed Chunk up in the practice arena. After he finished, to clear his mental cobwebs and get his head into the game, he rode Chunk to a field behind the rodeo grounds, a place where the cheers of the crowd faded, and the announcer sounded a world away.

Time must've gotten away from him because the next thing Levi knew, Cooter had ridden out to the edge of the field and whistled for him. He glanced up, and Cooter hitched a thumb over his shoulder toward the arena.

Levi put his heels to Chunk's sides and started trotting back. To save time, he cut through the outdoor pens where the roughstock were kept.

Olivia worked the chutes off to his right in preparation for the steer wrestling. A man with a little girl—maybe two or three-years-old—carried a small suitcase, his other hand wrapped firmly around the girl's wrist, half dragging her along.

"Ollie, Ollie." The little girl broke free from the man's grasp and ran toward Olivia.

A husband? No, the kid hadn't called her mommy. A boyfriend then?

Olivia looked up, confusion on her face, and happiness—then she saw the man and froze.

The man didn't look as much happy to see Olivia as he looked relieved. She caught the little girl up in her arms and held her tight to her chest, giving the kid a kiss on the top of her head. Levi turned away and headed for the main arena.

"What the hell are you doing here, Randy?" Olivia's voice carried over the rattle and clank of the chutes and the bawling of the cattle. The distress in her voice had Levi turning his horse in the aisle to watch. Something wasn't right.

The man, or Randy, apparently, tried to hand Olivia the suitcase, but she refused to take it. Randy's face turned the color of the pickled beets Levi's grandma always ate. He dumped the suitcase at her feet.

The girl cried out, "No, no. Dat mine!"

Levi pushed Chunk into a trot and rode up to Olivia. "Is there a problem?"

No one answered him or looked his way except for the waif of a girl with blond ringlets around her head like a living halo. The girl squealed, her face lighting up at the sight of Chunk. "Horsey, horsey."

Olivia ignored the kid, and him, but held on tight as the girl struggled to be put down. "You can't do this," Olivia said to Randy.

"You're right," Randy said, "I *can't* do this. I tried. I can't."

"You promised."

The girl put her little hands on Olivia's face to get her undivided attention. "Ollie, there's a horsey."

"Clementine, baby, please—"

"I no baby. Look." She turned Olivia's head until Chunk and Levi were in Olivia's line of sight. "Horsey."

Levi dismounted, looking Randy up and down, the man's face somehow familiar, yet not. Always good with names and faces, Levi was certain he'd never met the man before.

"You need me to get rid of this guy?" Levi asked Olivia.

One of Olivia's stockmen waved his hat to get her attention

and called out, "We've got to get the steers to the arena. We're holding up the show."

"Give me a second," Olivia hollered back. Then she tried to hand the little girl back to Randy. The guy backed away, his hands up, his eyes wide as if she held a rattlesnake in her hands, not a little girl. "Randy, you can't do this. You promised your sister." Her words came out more like a plea.

"That's what I've been trying to tell you. I just *can't*. It's past time her father stepped up." Randy turned and walked away.

Clementine made grabby hands toward Chuck, leaning so far out of Olivia's arm's Levi worried she'd take a tumble. He stuck a hand out to catch her if she fell.

"Marsh," another one of Olivia's stockmen called out. "We've got to go!"

Olivia still hadn't answered Levi. He put his hand on her shoulders and turned her to him. "You want me to stop that guy?"

"What?" Olivia asked as if she'd only now realized he was standing there.

"That guy. Do you want me to stop him?"

By the stricken expression on her face, she needed a lot more than for Levi to stop Randy from leaving.

"Now, Marsh," the stockman called out again.

Despite her disdain for Levi, or maybe because of it, he wanted to help her. Almost needed her to let him help. Maybe he had an untapped masochistic side. "What's going on?" Levi asked. "What do you need?"

Olivia shoved Clementine into his arms and to Levi's horror said, "I need you to take your daughter."

OLIVIA STRODE OVER TO THE CHUTES AND STARTED OPENING GATES

and herding the steers on through. Levi chased after her with Clementine in his arms.

A part of her felt guilty dumping Clementine on him like that, but what made her feel even more guilty was the sense of relief. Clementine wasn't Olivia's responsibility, and though Mae had extracted a promise from Randy under duress to take care of Clementine if anything were to happen to her, Clementine really wasn't Randy's responsibility either.

Now that Mae was gone, it was long past time for Clementine's father to step up to the plate. What was worse, Levi hadn't even recognized his own kid. The pictures Mae had sent him of Clementine had to be almost a year or so old. Sure, Clementine had grown and changed, that's what kids did, but she was far from unrecognizable. Not with Mae's big blue eyes, that shock of bright, blond hair, and that heart-melting smile.

"Olivia. *Olivia.*" Levi caught up with her, catching a hand around her elbow, forcing her to stop. He tried to hand Clementine back, but the child clung to him like a little monkey. "You have a lot of explaining to do."

"I think it's pretty self-explanatory. Unless your daddy didn't tell you that old story about the birds and the bees." She turned up the volume on her sarcasm. "You see when a boy loves a girl, he puts his—"

"Fuck. I know how it works, Liv."

"It's Olivia."

"Fuck, fuck, fuck, fuck," Clementine parroted like a salty old macaw.

"Baby, that's not a nice word," Levi said.

"Fuckity, fuck, fuck."

"They're sponges at this age," Olivia said. "You've got a watch your language."

Levi's expression laid flat on his face. "Clearly."

"Marsh," a stockman called out. "You trying to get your contract canceled?"

"I've got to go." Olivia kissed Clementine on her soft cheek and said to the little girl, "Be good."

When she walked away again, Levi called out, but he didn't chase after her. "What am I supposed to do? I've got to ride."

Olivia turned, walking backward down the aisle. "You do what everyone else in her life has done. You deal."

2

YOU DEAL. OLIVIA'S WORDS RATTLED AROUND LEVI'S BRAIN. HE didn't know what kind of sick joke Olivia was playing but he'd *deal* with her after his run.

Levi tried to put Clementine down and have her walk with him while he led Chunk. But herding a hundred feral cats would have been easier. She darted after everything that caught her eye.

After the second time he took something filthy from her hand, Levi decided to change things up.

"All right, Pix," Levi said, shortening pixie for a nickname. It seemed to suit her since she was as light as a fairy and nearly as dainty. How the hell could anyone believe that a man his size could father a kid so tiny? If she even was his kid. Seriously, he'd been careful to the point of obsession.

He picked her up and swung her into his saddle, her frilly pink dress floated down to her knees, her pint-size pink cowgirl boots hitting her mid-shin. She giggled and laughed and held on tight to the horn.

Chunk turned his head around and sniffed the tip of her

boot. Clementine wiggled in the saddle and slapped her hand on the cantle behind her. "Giddy up, horsey."

Chunk stared at Levi with his big brown eyes as if to say, "*Really?*"

Levi clucked to him and started walking again. Clementine squealed and laughed as Levi clamped a hand around her ankle to make sure she didn't slip off. What the hell was he going to do with her when he had to compete?

Beneath the stands, the concourse was thick with horses and competitors coming and going, the din of the echoing voices making it difficult to hear. He had to keep glancing over at Clementine to make sure the loud noises didn't scare or upset her, but the grin that balled up her cheeks told him that she was dealing with the situation much better than he was.

From atop his horse, she gave anyone who passed by a little princess wave, the kind the teen girls gave when circling the arena after being crowned rodeo princess. Had the kid ever met a stranger?

"Hey, Levi." Ian Murphy called out to him from his perch on top of the chutes. The rodeo photographer raised his ever-present camera and snapped a shot of Clementine on Chunk. "You're starting to date them a little young, aren't you?"

Levi couldn't help but chuckle. "You got a minute?" If Levi didn't hurry, he'd miss his go-round.

Ian climbed off the rails and dropped to the ground, capping his lens. "For you, buddy, anything."

Chunk halted when Levi stop walking. He tossed his reins over his horse's head and lifted Clementine from the saddle. "I need you to watch her until I'm finished riding. Her name is Clementine."

Ian gave him a funny look, somewhere between incredulity and oh-hell-no.

"I can explain," Levi said, then realized he was essentially in the dark as well. As soon as he caught up with Olivia, he'd drag the information out of her if he had to. "Actually, I can't. At least not yet."

Squatting down, he told Clementine, "I need you to stay with my friend, Ian. I'll be back real soon, and then we'll get something to eat. Okay?"

Clementine nodded. "Otay." She reached up and took hold of Ian's pinkie finger.

Ian turned green around the gills. "This isn't funny, man."

"You're telling me."

"I don't know anything about taking care of kids."

"You think I do?"

"What if she needs her diaper changed?" Panic crept into Ian's voice.

Levi didn't even know if she wore diapers. The fact he'd never thought to ask screamed at how bad he was at taking care of little humans.

To Clementine, he asked, "Do you wear diapers?"

She shook her head and pulled up the hem of her dress, exposing her matching pink panties. "I wears big girl panties."

"You can't show your panties in public," Levi said.

"But they's pwetty." Clementine raised her dress again to show him. Then she turned so Ian could see. "Pink is for pwincesses."

Ian glanced away, sweat breaking out on his forehead even as he tried to suppress his amusement, but a grin slipped free. "You heard her. Pink is for *pwincesses*." Ian purposely mangled the pronunciation. "You can't argue with that logic."

"Give me twenty minutes. Thirty tops. And I'll come back and find you."

"Don't leave me hanging, man."

"I promise I'll be right back." That is if he couldn't find a deep, dark hole to climb into. Somehow, someway, someone had made a huge mistake.

He'd get this sorted.

He had to.

As he waited his turn, his brain started putting the pieces together. If Olivia thought Clementine was his kid, it didn't take much mental calculation by a rocket scientist, or even a simple, homegrown steer wrestler to figure out Mae was the kid's mother. Now that the initial shock had worn off and his brain had kind of kicked back in, that was the only reasonable conclusion.

Which might explain why Olivia thought he was such an asshole, dead-beat dad. Well her ire needed to be pointed at the kid's real father, *not* him.

Knowing Mae, there was no telling how many lies she'd fed Olivia. Quite a few, from the looks of it.

Anger replaced his lingering grief over Mae's death. How could Mae do that to him? More importantly, how could she lie to an innocent child?

Levi's ride finished in a blur, his increasing anger pushing him harder. Chunk was on the steer in minimal strides, and Levi had his hands around the horns, taking them to the ground in record time. In fact, his personal best.

But he couldn't take any pleasure in it, not when fury fueled him.

Cooter walked over leading his horse. He clapped Levi on the shoulder. "Damn fine run, son."

Shaking the man's hand, Levi forced enthusiasm into his voice. "Couldn't do it without a good hazer."

"Ain't nothin'." Then Cooter focused on Levi, and the congratulatory smile slipped off the old codger's face. "Still having woman problems?"

Levi pulled his reins from around Chunk's neck. "Yeah, and I think they just doubled."

———

BACK AT HER MOTEL ROOM LATER THAT NIGHT, OLIVIA FINISHED the peanut butter sandwich she'd made for dinner. It was about time to check on Levi and Clementine and see how they'd fared for the evening.

While she was still pissed at Randy for taking advantage of the local stop on the rodeo's tour to dump Clementine on her, she had to keep in mind that Randy *had* lasted almost a year—months longer than she'd expected.

After Mae had died, Olivia had bet Randy wouldn't last a day, but he'd surprised her. Today, she'd put Levi to the test. She'd have to see if Levi would make it past the twenty-four-hour mark before he cried uncle as well.

A knock came at her motel room door. She brushed the time-worn, paper-thin curtains aside and peeked out. Rusty Dennard. Good guy. Smart guy. Crappy rodeo cowboy.

Olivia released the door chain, flipped the lock, and opened the door. "Hey, Rusty."

"Evening, ma'am." Rusty had his best cowboy hat in his hand. He only wore it out to the bars, though he didn't smell like he'd been drinking. "Sorry to be bothering you so late."

"It's not that late, and you're almost ten years older than I am. You don't have to call me ma'am."

"Yes, ma'am." Rusty's smile turned apologetic. "Sorry, ma'am."

Olivia waved him off. "It's fine. I don't mind. I just didn't want you feeling obligated."

"I appreciate that, ma'am."

"You can't help yourself. Can you?"

His toothy grin spread, the tips of his lips turning up. "No, ma'am."

Opening the door wider, Olivia stepped back and invited him in. Rusty kicked the dirt off his boots against the door sill and stepped over the threshold, a few early-season mosquitoes following him in.

Rusty took the chair at the small table in front of the window, and Olivia sat across from him on the bed. She really needed to check on Clementine. She made a get-on-with-it gesture with her hand. "What can I do for you, Rusty? "

"I'm done. With the rodeo. With bronc riding. As much as I wanted to be like my daddy, I don't have what it takes to be a champion. Besides, it's hard to live up to a ghost."

Olivia didn't know what to say. It wasn't like they were friends, though he'd ridden plenty of No Bull stock over the years. "I'm sorry to hear that, but what does that have to do with me?"

"I can't hardly feed my wife and kid on what I make on the circuit. Hell, I can hardly feed myself. It's time I got a real job and stopped chasing the dream my daddy had for me." Rusty fiddled with the snakeskin band around the crown of his hat, then glanced back up at her, his gaze somehow both solemn yet determined. "This is me, asking for a job."

Before she could ask him any questions, his nervousness must have gotten the better of him because he started making a case for himself. "Look, I know you've been in a bind since..."

"You can say it. Since Scottie Hines was arrested for assaulting Cora."

"I didn't want to beat a dead horse." He gave her a sorry-about-the-shitty-employee kind of shrug. "Thought you might need a new guy. I can haul the animals. I can do the logbooks. I can clean. I can feed. I'm good with animals. Good with a wrench. Hell, I'll do anything you need. I know you already got guys who can do Scottie's job. I'm not asking for that. I just need something steady. A paycheck my family can count on."

While Bob Forney and Jim Thomas were dependable, hard-working guys, part of the reason she was still on the road with the roughstock was that those men weren't exactly Harvard material. To make matters worse, she really needed to get back to the ranch before the calves and foals were born.

"Tell you what," Olivia said, "why don't you show up at the stockyard at six tomorrow morning? Starting wages. I pay on Fridays. No promises for anything permanent, but I'll give you a shot."

Rusty let out a heavy breath. He glanced away and swallowed hard, and stuck out his hand for her to shake, his voice still rough when he said, "Thanks. I won't let you down."

"No," Olivia said, with confidence, "I don't believe you will."

———

LEVI SAT AT THE DINETTE IN THE SHELL CAMPER ON HIS PICKUP truck and nursed a beer that had gone warm while he'd put an over-tired three-year-old to sleep. Exactly, how had he ended up with a tiny human his bed?

He had so many questions for Olivia, but she'd disappeared by the time he'd cooled Chunk down and had a chance go searching for her.

Leaning against the back wall, he watched the little girl sleep. How the hell had everyone in this girl's life failed her? How could her uncle dump her? Where were her grandparents? More importantly, where was Clementine's real father?

If Levi ever got his hands on the bastard who'd left her behind, the man might barely survive. Or at least, wish he hadn't.

Now that the kid was still for longer than one-point-five seconds, he could get a good, long look at her.

She was thin. Too thin. Most three-year-olds he'd known had rolls of fat on their arms and legs. Her dress was too small, too worn, too threadbare and her little boots had left blisters on her pinched toes. After the long day they'd both had, he'd been too tired to tackle the much-needed bath and, good Lord, the tangles in her hair.

He would never let his horse's mane and tail get that knotted, much less a child's.

Someone knocked on his door. Clementine startled but didn't wake. He turned the knob and pushed open the door from where he sat. With a truck camper, nothing was ever more than an arm's length away.

The rear leaf springs of his old truck creaked and groaned as Olivia stepped up into the camper, closing the door with a bang. Levi put a finger to his lips and pointed to Clementine.

"Sorry," she mouthed.

Removing his feet from the seat across from him, he motioned for her to sit.

She squeezed in and whispered, "How does a man your size fit in here? I barely fit."

"You're not exactly height-challenged, for a woman."

"True, but you're—"

"Cramped. But it's better than sleeping in my truck or sharing a motel room with three or four other guys to keep the cost down."

"Hey," she said. "I get it. If I had an option besides a motel, I'd be doing that, too. Paying for an extra room every night is eating into my profits."

He gave her a non-committal smile. After the day he'd had, Olivia's cost of doing business didn't even ping on his radar. If that made him an uncaring bastard, he'd gladly take the moniker and have it tattooed in red on his forehead.

"You don't want to hear about my problems," she said. "Do you?"

"Not particularly." He spared her a thin chuckle. That was all he had the mental energy for. "I want to know how I ended up with a toddler in my trailer."

"Your daughter's almost three, so technically, I'm not sure you can call her a toddler."

"Toddler. Kid. Call her what you want, but I can't call her mine."

Olivia's face turned pink, then red as anger burned and bordered on fury. "You are such a bastard, how—"

Levi reached across the table and clapped a hand over Olivia's mouth. Clementine whimpered in her sleep.

In a whisper-shout, he said, "Would you keep your voice down? I got her to sleep not twenty minutes ago."

"*Oomph*," she said from behind his hand.

But before he could ask her if she was going to keep her voice down, she bit his finger. Hard. He snatched his hand back.

"Ouch, motherfu—"

"No cussing," she said from behind a grin she couldn't hide. "Little ears."

He sucked on the meat of his finger, and her eyes locked on for a bit too long, her tongue raking across her bottom lip. If she had been any other woman, he might have read it as a sign that she was interested. But this was Olivia. The woman who despised him. And if he had any doubt, he could look at the incisor indentations on his finger for proof.

"Are you current on your shots, or am I going to have to have animal control put you in quarantine?"

"Very funny." She wasn't laughing. "How's it going?"

She wasn't asking about his injury. Ignoring her question, he hitched his thumb over his shoulder at the camper door. The thought of waking Clementine when their voices got raised—which would be inevitable with them—terrified him. He couldn't remember the last time he'd been that exhausted, and he'd only had the kid for a handful of hours.

How did parents manage with their kids day in and day out?

He had to seriously rethink the whole idea of having kids of his own someday because he might not be cut out to be a dad.

Levi held the door open and followed Olivia out, catching a whiff of her as she passed. She smelled of cattle, and hay, and pine shavings, and hard work. Not roses or flowery perfume. It shouldn't have turned him on, but that combination of scents on her hit him like some sort of Wild West aphrodisiac.

He couldn't let it go to his little head. This was Olivia, after all.

Leaving the door open a smidge in case Clementine woke up, Levi retrieved two fold-out chairs laying against his back bumper and wrestled them open.

"Sit," he said. It wasn't a request.

Olivia was slow to sit, but she sat.

Levi placed the other chair directly in front of her and settled in. It was past time he got to the bottom of this. He leaned forward, his elbows on his knees. "Start from the beginning."

"You were there, you should know."

Levi scrubbed his hands through his hair. "She. Is. Not. Mine."

"Yes," Olivia said, matching his emphatic tone. "She. Is."

"How do you know?"

"Because Mae said so. Why would she lie?"

"Because she always lies. You can believe me or not, but she never told me about Clementine. Hell, she never told me she was pregnant."

"What about the photos of Clementine she sent?"

"She never sent any photos. If she was willing to lie to you about the photos and even that fact that she'd told me, what makes you think she wouldn't lie about me being the father?"

Olivia leaned back, her expression wary and contemplative. "She really never told you?"

"No." Levi allowed a huff of frustration to leak into his voice. "And it wouldn't have mattered that she and I were no longer together. I wouldn't have run off and left her to manage with a kid her own. *If* Clementine were my kid. Which she's not."

"Clementine's birthday is in two weeks. She'll be three. Count back nine months from there."

Between the exhaustion and the beer, it took him a minute to count back. "That puts conception mid '72. We'd already broken up by then."

"July 1972. Unless she was lying about that trip you two took to—"

Shit. "The Grand Canyon. She caught up with me right after the summer rodeo season had ended. She wanted to get back together. That weekend was a disaster. We learned there was a good reason why we'd broken it off."

"But you two had sex."

He couldn't believe he was talking about his sex life with Mae's cousin, the woman who'd probably give a steer extra rations if it gored him in the gut as he wrestled it to the ground.

Could Clementine really be his?

"Our sex life was never an issue. It was the time we spent out of bed that was the problem. Especially when she brought illegal drugs into the mix. We only had sex one time that weekend."

"It only takes one time."

Olivia had tenacity. A quality he could admire if it hadn't been focused on him. "Who's to say she didn't sleep with someone right before or right after we'd been together and only claimed the baby was mine?"

Olivia glared at him with an expression that called him seven kinds of idiot. "We both know Mae was many things, but promiscuous wasn't one of them. Not until much later. After the baby came. When she couldn't deal. When the drugs became more than recreational."

He took Olivia's words in. Mulled them over. If what Olivia said was true, he'd have to at least consider the possibility, but how could he know for certain?

Was he a father?

If today had been any indication, he wasn't cut out for fatherhood. At least not at this stage in his life.

Olivia snapped her fingers in front of his face. "You didn't hear a word I said, did you?"

Levi stared down at the gravel between his feet. "I was too busy freaking the fuck out. What did you say?"

"I *said* if Mae had named you as the father only because she wanted something from you, why wouldn't she tell you about Clementine?"

The urge to reach for another beer or something stronger until his problems disappeared seemed overwhelming, but getting blackout drunk was not an option, not until he figured out what he was going to do about the kid.

Leaning back, he said, "You're making a lot of sense."

"Thank you."

"What for?"

"For admitting that. I know it had to be painful for you."

Did she tease him?

Her mouth quirked up at the edges, dislodging a begrudging chuckle from him. "You have no idea."

They lapsed into silence. He had a lot to absorb. Olivia slouched down in her chair, stretched her long legs out in front of her, and stared up at a jet-black sky dotted with an infinite number of stars, apparently content to leave him to his thoughts.

She could have left at that point, but she didn't, and he appreciated that.

"What about Mae's parents? Surely they would be a better—"

Olivia laughed, more derisive then humorous. "Mae wouldn't allow Clementine anywhere near her parents. She figured they screwed her up enough, there was no way she'd allow her parents to do the same to their granddaughter."

Again, silence filled the gap before Olivia spoke again. "Mae tried so hard to do it on her own. She'd even kicked the drugs for a while, trying to be strong in her own way, but her self-doubt and her demons got the best of her. The downward spiral was slow, almost unnoticeable as she compensated. Then..." Olivia shrugged. "Then it wasn't. Then it was too late."

Anger rose. A rising tide that swelled and grew and threatened to swamp him. Standing, he paced back and forth before his emotions—the disbelief, the regret, the guilt—drowned him. He turned back toward Olivia, his throat tight. "Why didn't she say something? Why didn't she ask for my help?"

"You broke her heart, Levi."

"I tried to get her help, I—"

"I know. She told me. It crushed her when you walked away. She couldn't or wouldn't go crawling back. No matter what."

"Then you, or someone else, should have told me."

"I didn't know the truth until the end. Even then, she made me promise I wouldn't tell."

"But you did. You had to have told her brother, otherwise he wouldn't have known where to find me."

"That was a mistake."

So, so, so much anger. At Mae. At her family. At Olivia. At himself. But for the life of him, he couldn't think how he could have done things any differently that would have made the situation better.

He turned his wrath on her because she was within striking distance. "If Randy hadn't come, if Randy hadn't had enough, you would have let me, let Clementine, go our whole lives without knowing the other existed?"

Olivia stood and got in his face. "Don't blame me, or anyone else besides Mae and yourself. *She's* the one who lied. *You're* the one that burned the bridge and scorched the earth around it, making her feel like you were the last person she could turn to." She thumped him in the chest with the palm of her hand, her eyes glittered in the dark, full of piss and vinegar and indignant outrage. "That's not on me."

Levi fell back a step. Blowing out a scalding breath, he raised his hands in defeat and came right out and admitted the truth in what she'd said, "You're right."

"What kind of man—" Olivia gave her head a shake as if she couldn't believe what she'd heard.

He was surprised she didn't stick a finger in her ear and wiggle it around to make sure she wasn't hearing things.

"Wait, you said I was right?"

"I did."

Olivia almost looked disappointed. It made him smile.

"Why are you smiling?"

"You're kind of sexy when your protective mama bear comes out."

3

———————

Sexy? Levi Banks thought she was sexy? Maybe being hit with the fact he was a father had somehow affected his vision. Men usually found her protective streak overbearing and patently unflattering.

As much as she wished for a witty comeback, Olivia couldn't think of one. In its place, an unsexy, undignified, uncharacteristic, "Uhhhh..." came out.

She'd had it in for this man since Mae had told her he was Clementine's father. That night Mae had been strung out, trying for the umpteenth time to quit drugs cold turkey.

God, Mae had tried, but in the end, her pain, her addiction, won.

And now... And now everything Olivia thought she knew about this man could be utterly, completely, life-changingly wrong.

Maybe if she considered him an ally and not the enemy, they could do what needed to be done—make sure Clementine grew up happy, healthy, and above everything else, loved.

"At least I know how to make you shut up. All I have to do is tell you you're right," Levi said.

"That I'm right should be a given." Except when she was wrong. The way she'd been wrong about Levi. "You're still an asshole," Olivia said, but the begrudging smile she couldn't fight off probably took the sting out of her words.

Levi's grin got wider.

"That wasn't a compliment."

"When it's said without venom, it almost sounds like a term of endearment. I think you like me, Olivia Marsh."

Olivia scoffed. Just because the guy was hot and maybe not the complete and utter rotten bastard that Mae had made him out to be didn't mean she liked him. He had a long way to go in her book to make it past asshole.

They yawned at the same time. Both had had a long day, and the emotional roller coaster only made the day that much more exhausting.

"Do you want help setting up a pallet for Clementine to sleep on?"

"I laid her on the bed. It's big enough for both of us."

"That's cute."

"What's that?"

Besides the way his brows locked together when he scowled? "You've never slept with a three-year-old, have you?"

"I don't normally make a habit of it, no."

"They kick, they punch, they lay over your head like a cat in heat. You won't get any sleep with her in the bed."

"You've seen the camper. It's not like I've got a spare room stacked up in there. What you see is what you get."

Olivia opened his door and whispered, "Come on, I'll help you get her situated."

In the end, they turned the kitchen table and dinette into a bed for Clementine. It was too short and narrow for an adult, but for Clementine, it would be perfect. Levi used an extra blanket for bedding and gave her his spare pillow.

When Olivia went to move her, Levi put a staying hand on her shoulder and said, "I've got her."

Clementine woke when Levi lifted her to his chest and rubbed at her eyes.

"Ollie," Clementine said.

"Hey, baby." Olivia reached for Clementine, but the little girl snuggled deeper against Levi's chest, her little arms tight around his neck.

"I no go with Randy. Me want Lebi."

"Oh, baby," Olivia said, stroking her hair. "I'm not taking you away. It's okay."

Clementine had never been a shy kid, but the way she'd taken to Levi in a few short hours made Olivia's heart pinch and her chest tighten.

She'd thought leaving Clementine with Randy had been for the best. That's what Mae had wanted, but it had taken Clementine months before she'd warmed up to Randy. It had taken Levi one night. Which compounded the guilt she now felt for not telling Levi about his daughter. For both of their sakes.

But you'd promised.

Yeah. Look where that had gotten them. And it had been Clementine who'd unknowingly paid the price. Not that Randy had been cruel. More like indifferent.

A child as sweet and innocent as Clementine deserved to be loved like a precious gift, not tolerated like a heavy burden.

With care, Levi laid Clementine on the bed and tucked the light-weight blanket around her. Her eyes rolled into the back of her head, but her little arm raised, her hand making a grabbing motion.

"Her horsey," Levi said. He squeezed past Olivia and retrieved Clementine's stuffed horsey and placed it under her arm. He leaned down and pressed a tender kiss to her temple. "Night, night, Pix."

"Night," Clementine muttered.

Levi shut off the overhead light, letting the tiny single bulb over his two-burner stove act as a nightlight.

They both climbed back out of the camper, and again Levi left the door ajar, surprising Olivia with his thoughtfulness and consideration.

Maybe there was more to this man than the bad things Mae had told her. He'd turned on his yellow bug light next to his door as he'd come out. In the amber glow, he didn't look like he had the answers. Before she could step away, he reached for her hand, gently snagging her pinkie finger and pulling her closer.

Not enough that their bodies touched, but enough that they shared the same space and proximity, his voice slow and cautious when he said, "I don't know what I'm doing." The stark vulnerability made her want to wrap him in her arms and make it better. Make the mistakes and broken hearts go away. But she couldn't fix the past.

"You'll figure it out." She didn't say it to be dismissive, she said it with a faith she believed. Where that faith had come from, she didn't know—maybe from the tender way he'd held Clementine, or the way he already had a nickname for her, or maybe because he'd known that when Clementine had reached out that she'd needed her horsey—but that's why it's called faith, and not certainty.

"You say that like you believe it." He sounded like he wanted to believe it too.

Levi Banks wasn't an evil entity to loathe. He was simply a man, doing his best to come to terms with his new reality. Olivia couldn't fault him for that.

Olivia cupped his cheek. Because she was already there, standing so close, she leaned into him and pressed a kiss to his cheek. "That's because I do."

———

THREE WEEKS LATER, LEVI BRUSHED THE DIRT OFF HIS JEANS, AND glanced up at his time on the scoreboard of the Terrebonne Parrish fairgrounds, near Houma, Louisiana. The crowd roared as Levi raised his hat in salute. He gathered Chunk's reins and swung back up into the saddle and rode out of the arena, the irony already sinking in that he'd never posted such consistently good times as he'd had since Clementine had come into his life. The wins meant less to him than they ever had, except for the fact he could more easily provide for his daughter.

Everyone on the circuit had been calling her his good luck charm, and a few had even sought her out before their runs for a good luck fist bump, hoping the luck would wear off on them.

But the truth was, Levi was too scared to fail, to fail her. The rodeo was what he knew, and it was his only means of support.

Now instead of going to the bars on Sunday nights to celebrate winning a check, he stuck close to the camper or he took Clementine to a local diner for a late-night ice cream.

Once clear of the alley, Levi dismounted and led Chunk toward the concession stand where he'd left Clementine with Olivia.

"Chunky!" Clementine called out.

Levi glanced up to see Ian walking toward him, his camera slung around his neck and Clementine's hand gripped in his. She pulled Ian the entire way, like a little dog on a short leash.

Chunk stopped and lowered his head, and Clementine hugged his face and gave him a kiss on his wide forehead before letting go.

"Hey, Pix." Levi patted her back when she wrapped her arms around his leg.

"Me ride Chunky."

"In a minute." Levi turned his attention to Ian. He stuck out his hand for the other man to shake. "Thanks for watching her. I thought Olivia was on munchkin duty."

Ian shrugged as if it were no big deal, even though Levi knew Ian had to have missed many shots of the rodeo while his friend babysat his kid. "One of the bulls came up lame, so Olivia had to meet with the vet."

"Well, I owe you one. Hell, I think I owe everyone by now. You, Cora, Josephine, Olivia, and half of the regular competitors. Everyone has been so great pitching in when I've needed it. I've been trying to find a reliable babysitter, but so far that hasn't proven easy."

"That's what friends are for. We're here for each other."

"Yeah, but this is more than letting me borrow a few bucks or checking on my horse."

"She's a terrific kid. We're happy to help."

Even though Levi couldn't take the credit, his chest swelled with pride. "Yeah, she is kind of amazing." Levi clapped Ian on the shoulder. "Well, thanks again. You better get going before you miss the good shots."

"Will do." Ian started walking away, then stopped and said, "Cora and I are having a little get together at our camper tonight after the rodeo. Bring the kid."

Speaking of kids, Clementine was busy walking between Levi's legs going around and around and around. He took her hand, and she leaned against it, one foot on the ground the other trying to climb up his leg. "Thanks. We'll try to be there if Clementine isn't too worn out."

"One beer at least," Ian insisted. "I'm sure a little adult company will do you good. Besides, you can always lay her down in my camper if she's tired. And Olivia said she'd be there..."

Adult conversation. An adult beverage...and Olivia? An offer too good to pass up. "I'll do that. Thanks."

After Ian left, Levi grabbed Clementine up to peals of laughter as he swung her up and into his saddle, her new pink boots dangling on either side of his horse, her matching pink hat down low on her forehead.

Chunk's ears turned backward waiting for her command. Clementine clucked, and Chunk took one cautious step and then another until Levi started walking. Who would have thought that the gelding that had taken extra-long to break because he had a bucking issue would treat his kid like precious cargo?

Back at the stalls after cooling Chunk down, Levi plopped Clementine on a bale of hay while he untacked and took care of his horse for the night.

She stood on the bale, shaking her booty to a song stuck in her head. If she was tired, she wasn't showing signs of it yet, her natural night-owl shining through.

Hopefully when it came time to go to Ian and Cora's, she'd be conked out.

He went to open Chunk's stall, and Clementine said, "Lemme do it."

She jumped down from the bale and reached for the door latch but was too short to reach. When he went to help, she batted his hand away. "Me, me."

Levi backed off a step and chuckled to himself. "Okay, Einstein, let's see you figure this out."

She jumped, but with a vertical leap of half an inch, it didn't help much. Then she took her own step back and looked at the door then at the bale of hay beside it. She tried to slide the bale over, but only managed to grunt and groan and pull out stray strands of hay.

"You want help?"

She slid him a look. That same look Mae used to give him when he would ask a dumb question.

Then Clementine climbed back on the bale, grabbed the vertical bars at the top third of the stall, and using her hands and feet, slowly worked her way over to the latch, her booted feet slipping and sliding against the solid wood walls.

Clementine almost fell twice, but those skinny little arms were stronger than they looked. At the latch, she braced her feet and let go with one hand long enough to flip the latch open.

Then she jumped the two feet down, landing hard and falling on her butt. She rolled to her hands and knees and stood, wiping the dirt off on her dress. With two hands, she pushed on the sliding door. It stuck halfway, but it was enough for her.

She turned and hit him with a megawatt smile that lit the grin on his own face.

He gave her a fist bump. "Look at you."

"Told you," she said, full of sass and herself.

"Okay, back on the hay bale where it's safe."

She scrambled out of the stall, climbing on the bale, and staring through the bars. He never allowed Clementine in the stall with Chunk. Especially when the horse wasn't haltered. It wasn't that he didn't trust Chunk with Clementine. The horse had proven that he wouldn't try to hurt her. But he was a thousand pounds of prey animal. If something spooked him, she could get trampled by accident and Levi wouldn't take that kind of chance.

After topping off Chunk's hay and water, Levi crouched down low enough for Clementine to climb onto his back and wrap her arms around his neck.

"You hungry, Pix?"

"I want hot dogs."

"We had hot dogs last night. And two nights before that. How about grilled cheese and apples and—"

Clementine squeezed him with her legs the way she did with Chunk, giving him a cluck and an enthusiastic, "Giddy up."

"I'm going, I'm going." Levi chuckled.

"Faster, Lebi!"

Levi sped up, adding a bounce in his step. She giggled and laughed, the sound going straight to his heart, making his chest ache. He thought his life has been full before, but he'd had no idea what he'd been missing until Clementine came along. The days were certainly longer, the worry was greater, but watching the way her eyes lit up when she saw him righted his crooked world.

Levi had always imagined that when he had kids, he'd be married, have a place to come home to the wife and kid after the long weeks on the circuit.

He'd never pictured going it alone.

Or living out of a pickup camper with a three-year-old.

Now he couldn't imagine anything different.

"Faster, faster," Clementine commanded, one arm flailing behind her as she pretended to whip him.

"Remind me never to buy you spurs," he said as he broke into a jog. When he got to Ian's, he hoped to get Olivia alone and find out why the hell she'd been avoiding him.

———

AT CORA AND IAN'S CAMPER, PARKED IN THE BACK LOT OF THE Terrebonne Parish fairgrounds grounds, five rigs over from his own, Levi settled into one of the folding chairs Ian had laid out for the get-together.

Ian and Cora had a camper trailer, complete with a bed in the back and a wraparound kitchen table in the front. It wasn't huge, but compared to Levi's cab-over camper, it was positively spacious.

Their camper door had been latched open, the light from the kitchen spilling out. Levi crossed an ankle over his knee and laid a sleeping Clementine, dressed in her new pajamas with the galloping horses print, across his lap. Her head lay on his thigh and her little legs dangling over the side of the chair.

One of these days, he would have to learn to tell his kid no, but one look at those big, blue, beautiful eyes and those pouty lips, and the 'no' always turned to a 'yes.'

If his bulldogging buddies knew the truth, that a little girl could bring him to his knees with one pitiful look, they'd laugh their ever-lovin' asses off.

"Oh, hey," Cora called out from the camper in a half-whisper. "You made it."

"Hey." Levi used his normal voice. "It's okay, you don't have to whisper. I've discovered when she's exhausted like this, she can sleep through a hurricane."

"Hey, man." Ian stuck his head out, rather, his camera lens and flash and snapped a quick shot of the sleeping Clementine before putting the camera down. "We'll be right out."

"Where is everybody?"

"A few of the others changed their minds and decided to hit the bars. Josephine called it an early night, but I think Olivia is still planning on coming once she's done with the vet."

Fine with him. Ever since the kid came along, his hankering for heavy drinking and large, boisterous groups had pretty much died. These days, a quiet hour or two to himself after Clementine crawled into bed seemed like a damn luxury.

Jesus Christ. He was turning into his old man.

At least without a big audience, maybe he'd have a chance to take Olivia aside and find out what was up with her.

Cora clomped down the camper steps with a bottle of beer in each hand. She handed one to him and leaned in for a quick hug and a platonic peck on the cheek. Ian came out a second or two later, with his own beer and a small packed cooler so they wouldn't have to get up for their second round.

Across from him, Cora and Ian arranged two chairs next to each other, Cora sitting sideways in hers, her legs and bare feet over the arm, her head resting on Ian's shoulder as she sipped her beer.

He waited for that old pang to hit him. That pinch to his heart that reminded him that he hadn't completely gotten over her, but for once it didn't come. The affection remained, but the deep hurt felt like a distant memory. Had he finally accepted that he and Cora were never meant to be, or did that realization come as a certain someone came barreling into his life without so much as an apology?

Glancing down, he took in the sight of his daughter in his lap.

Yes. *His* daughter. He'd received the confirmation on Friday. He hadn't passed the news on. It had been something he'd wanted to keep to himself at least for a few days, not because he had to come to terms with it, but because it was something special he wanted to live between the two of them, even if for only a day or two.

He stared at the blond ringlets that he'd finally been able to detangle, and the pale, long lashes against clean cheeks that were finally filling out. He brushed his knuckle across her soft skin. He had another little lady in his life.

His heart pinched and his chest got tight as his heart swelled with love and pride for this perfect little girl.

"Oh my God," Cora said as she sat up. "You are *so* gone for that kid."

Levi waited for the flush of heat to rush up his neck, for embarrassment to hit him, but it never came. He glanced up, his gaze going from Cora's shocked expression to Ian's sly, knowing grin. "Can you blame me?"

"No, buddy," Ian said, taking a quick swig, "I can't."

Cora's eyes went soft, and she cupped Ian's cheek. "Our time will come," she told him. "Just not yet."

Ian kissed her palm and linked his hand with hers. "I'm not in any hurry, Sunshine. One of you is about all I can handle right now."

Cora gave him a playful swat on the arm. "You are such an ass—"

"Language," Levi said.

Ian chuckled. Cora let out an exasperated huff, and hissed, "She's asleep."

"She still hears *everything*. Trust me, you finish that word, and that's what she'll be calling everybody tomorrow."

"But it was so cute when she called Maynard Rowe a little s-h-i-t the other day," Cora said.

"She wasn't wrong," Ian allowed. "She gets extra points for using bad words in the correct context."

"That's beside the point." Levi couldn't help his grin. The rodeo manager hadn't thought it was as cute or funny as the rest of them had. "You guys laughed, and that's the only thing she said for the next hour."

Cora settled back against Ian and bobbed her chin toward Clementine. "So how is fatherhood? Really?"

The grin slipped from Levi's face. Ian and Cora had come to be his closest friends. Besides Olivia, those two had helped him the most since Clementine had stormed into his life. If he couldn't tell them the truth...

"Complicated," was the word he settled on. "Trying. Exhausting," he added with a light laugh. "But also challenging, fun, and rewarding. I mean, I've always enjoyed other people's kids, but when they're *your* kid..."

Levi's throat got tight, and he shook his head. Cora and Ian could finish the sentence on their own.

It was Ian who broke the silence. "I guess you heard back from the doctor then?"

"And the lawyer," Levi said after clearing his throat. "Mae named me as the father on the birth certificate, so according to the law, I'm the father. But the doctor did a blood type test. According to medical records, Mae was A-. I'm B-. Both are found in only five to six percent of the population. Clementine is AB-. Only about one percent of the population has that blood type. It's not a hundred percent guarantee she's my kid, but considering the other circumstances, it's good enough for me."

Olivia came around the corner of the camper, retrieved a beer from the cooler and popped off the top on the edge of the foldout chair's arm. "Did I hear that right? She's really yours?"

"Unless science comes up with a better test that proves otherwise," Levi said. "Either way, I'm not giving her up."

"Here, here," Olivia said, clacking the bottom of her beer to his. "Congratulations, Dad. It's a girl."

Olivia leaned forward and brushed the damp, freshly showered locks from Clementine's forehead. "You and Mae might have mixed like oil and water, but you two sure made one hell—"

Levi made a *watch-it* sound.

"—*heck* of a kid."

Levi sent her a wink. Olivia looked away, but not before he caught the flush that ran up her cheeks.

"How's the bull?" Cora asked.

"He's got a hoof abscess that ruptured. I'm having Rusty take him back to the ranch tomorrow. He'll swap Dream Crusher out with another bull and meet us in Lufkin later in the week."

"It's that serious?" Levi brushed the condensation from his beer onto his jeans.

"Serious enough that I don't want him standing around in a small, mucky paddock. I need him where I can be sure the wound stays clean while he heals. I'd love to be the one who takes him back. I'm so tired of motels and concession stand food."

"At least with the stoves in the campers, we can attempt to make real food," Levi said. "Though Clementine would live on stale hot dogs and cotton candy, if I let her."

And nachos and French fries and funnel cakes.

The way she'd curled her nose up at the first apple he'd sliced for her, he would have thought she'd never seen a piece of fruit before.

Olivia granted him a smile. Her smiles had seemed so few and far between, especially when they'd been directed at him, that it almost seemed like a precious gift. "You're good for her."

Coming from the woman who a mere few weeks ago could barely stomach looking at him, he lapped up the compliment like lavish praise.

You're such a chump for a pretty face.

Yeah, but Olivia Marsh was so much more than a beautiful woman with a tight, toned body that made his dick hard and his brain go places he was convinced she'd never want to go.

But that's why they were called daydreams, not reality.

"Thanks," he said, holding her steady, sincere gaze.

His eyes went from hers to the curve of her upper lip and the way they bowed up at the edges when she saw him. The way they were doing now. He couldn't say that Olivia was his biggest fan, but her disdain had drained away.

When he glanced back up at her eyes, her gaze had shifted lower as well. She was interested.

Ian cleared his throat. "You want us to give you two some privacy?"

"Oh, heck, no." Cora said, "I've always liked a good fireworks show." Then she held her hands out and rubbed them together as if warming them at a fire. "I can feel the heat from here."

"*Cora.*" Ian's tone held admonishment, but the not-well-fought grin only encouraged her, the same way laughing at Clementine's use of cuss words only made her say them more.

"Seriously," Cora said, "I think I got first degree burns."

"Funny," Olivia deadpanned.

When the silence got awkward, Olivia drained the last of her beer and said, "I really should get back to the motel. Tomorrow's going to come early."

"Now you've done it," Ian said, his tone toward Cora still indulgent.

"Stay," Cora said. "Please, I didn't mean anything—"

"No, it's good." Olivia stood. "It's not you, it's—"

The three of them sat, waiting for her to finish her thought. Maybe she'd finally come out and say what was on her mind. Say what had been eating at her for the last couple weeks. But then she said, "It's late."

Levi didn't know Olivia that well yet, but well enough to tell when she was lying—okay, well not lying, since it *was* technically late—but omitting the truth. And he wasn't going to let her get away with it.

He shifted Clementine to his arms. "I'll walk you back to your truck. I should be putting her to bed anyway."

Levi stood and almost stumbled.

Ian scrambled to his feet and steadied Levi with a hand on his shoulder. "You okay, man?"

"Yeah, my leg fell asleep." He hissed in a breath. The pins and needles kicked in as sensation returned.

"Here, let me take her." Olivia held out her hands. When Levi hesitated, she added, "You never let me hold her anymore."

"You have her all the time," Levi corrected.

"I have her when she's awake and running me ragged, not when she's asleep and pretending to be an angel."

It wasn't that he had a problem letting Olivia hold her, it was that he hated to give Clementine up when she was all loose limbs and sweet sighs.

But if Olivia took her, it would be an excuse to get Olivia back to his place. Olivia, being Olivia, she didn't wait for him to answer. She took Clementine from his arms and laid his daughter against her shoulder. Clementine stirred but snuggled her face deeper against Olivia's neck and fell back asleep on that same tender spot on Olivia's neck Levi wanted to nip and taste.

"I was going to stop by your trailer. I've got something I need to talk to you about," Olivia said to Levi.

Her tone made Levi wary. Whatever she had to say couldn't be good if she were unwilling to say anything in front of Ian and Cora.

"Sure." Levi tried his best to sound unaffected and not like someone had poured a gallon of acid down his gullet.

Shaking Ian's hand, Levi said, "Thanks for the beer."

"I appreciate the invite," Olivia said, shifting her arms under Clementine's rump. "Jesus, Banks, what have you been feeding this kid? Concrete blocks?"

"Don't worry," Levi said. "I grind them up. It's easier on her teeth that way."

Olivia rolled her eyes, but he detected a hint of a smile. "Night, y'all."

"Night," Cora and Ian said as they started gathering up the chairs.

Levi followed Olivia and Clementine back to his camper, as the acid building in his gut ate at his stomach lining layer by layer. At this rate, by the time they made it back to his camper, he'd have a bleeding ulcer.

4

———

Levi's footfalls fell heavy on the asphalt parking lot. He practically breathed down Olivia's neck the whole way back to his truck.

She couldn't blame the Louisiana humidity for the thin layer of sweat moistening her hairline and dripping down between her breasts because it had everything to do with the news she had to tell him.

He held the camper door open for her and put a stabilizing hand on her arm as she climbed the steps. Giving the sleeping Clementine one last hug, she buried her nose in the little girl's hair and soaked up her scent before laying her down on her makeshift bed.

With no available space to sit in the camper, she stepped back and closed the screen door to keep the mosquitoes out.

The light from the camper spilled into the parking lot. Levi stood in front of her, arms across his chest, and a glower across his brow.

"Why does your daughter smell like *Mane 'n Tail* horse shampoo?"

Levi got a sheepish grin. "It's the only thing I could find that helped keep her hair from getting tangled during the day." Then his glance got assessing as if he knew something else was bothering her. He rubbed at the base of his neck. "This isn't about my shampoo choices. What's going on?"

Maybe she was making a bigger deal out of this than she needed to, maybe it was nothing to worry about at all.

"I talked to my grandfather this afternoon. Mae's parents called and left a message for him to pass along to me."

Levi's head came up, and his eyes narrowed. "What's the message?"

"They're coming to see Clementine next weekend when the rodeo swings through Lufkin."

Levi shrugged, and the tension left his body. "That's it? That's what's got you worked up?"

"I'm not worked up, I'm just..."

Levi raised a brow waiting for her to finish the sentence.

Instead, she said, "You've never met them. You don't know how they can be."

"I have an idea," Levi said. "Mae didn't have many good things to say about them from what I can remember. But Clementine's their granddaughter, their only link to the child they've lost. I can't refuse to let them see her."

"You can. You're her father. You—" She cut herself off. He really had no idea how bad Mae's parents could be. Her own parents had done their best to protect her from Mae's mother's toxicity, but sometimes you couldn't escape family. Especially since her mother and Mae's mother were sisters.

Olivia had a bad feeling. The kind of bad that made her stomach knot, her heart feel heavy, and left the bitter taste of bile sitting at the back of her throat.

"Hey, hey, hey." Levi closed the gap between them and peeled one of her hands free from where she'd wrapped it around herself. "It's okay. I'm not letting anything happen to Clementine. Trust me."

Shaking her head, Olivia said, "They destroyed Mae's life. They're wrecking balls wrapped up in Seersucker suits and double-knit polyester."

He trapped her palm against his chest right over his heart, the beat steady, strong, and true. "I protect what's mine, Olivia Marsh." He dropped his voice low, and she had to pay extra close attention to his words when he spoke. "You don't have to worry about us."

Then the rat bastard lifted her hand and pressed a scorching kiss to the palm. It was like he knew how much even his stray touches affected her. His voice went gruff when he said, "I appreciate you worrying about us. I assure you it's unnecessary."

She took her hand back and stuffed it into the front pocket of her jeans so he wouldn't notice her mild tremor. Her mouth had gone dry and her throat made an audible click when she swallowed. "Don't say I didn't warn you."

When she turned to walk away, he stopped her with a hand on her forearm. "You said that you talked to your grandfather today."

She faced him. "Yeah, this afternoon. Why?"

"Then having Clementine's grandparents come to visit doesn't explain why you've been avoiding me."

She hadn't exactly been avoiding him. Mostly. Okay. Maybe on some level... But her personal issues were her business. "What are you talking about? Is the lack of sleep catching up to you? I see you every day. I help you with Clementine, I—"

"True." He took a step closer. "Believe me, I appreciate the help. Having a three-year-old on the road isn't easy."

"That's why I'm helping."

"But this has nothing to do with that. You've hardly said two words to me that didn't have to do with caring for Clementine.

Am I really that bad of a person?" He said it with a grin, but the naked vulnerability lurked in his dark eyes.

She shook her head. She could admit that now. "That's the problem."

He laughed loud enough to wake Clementine, but she barely stirred. "You've completely lost me."

She couldn't look him in the eye, afraid he'd see the naked want she'd been trying to hide, but he put a finger under her chin and lifted her face to his. His thumb brushed against her bottom lip. Just a touch.

She needed to leave before she did something totally idiotic, like kiss him.

Or drag him into his camper and strip him naked.

"Tell me." Part command. Part request.

Rising on her toes, she placed her hand behind his neck and pulled him in for that kiss. She'd gone in for a quick, light touch. A sample. A taste.

But Levi took it deeper. He didn't devour her. He simply angled his head, a teasing touch of his tongue tracing the seam of her lips until she opened for him.

Their tongues touched, and she tasted the hops from his beer that somehow must have been more intoxicating than when it had been in the bottle because her head got light and the stars above began to spin.

A soft groan escaped his throat, and his hands traced down her sides and rested at the top of her ass.

What the hell was she doing? She broke the kiss. "I'm sorry, I didn't mean—"

She backed away a few steps, hoping to be able to draw in a breath of fresh air, but they weren't far from the Louisiana swamps, and the air was thick and heavy. At least that's what she told herself because it was the only logical explanation for the tightness in her chest. "I'll see you two tomorrow."

Spinning on her heel, she tried to make her escape, but Levi's big paw caught her again. "Oh no, you don't. Not so fast."

She stopped but didn't turn around. "Let me go, Banks."

He dropped his hand. "You can't kiss me like that and run, leaving me to wonder what's going on."

Fine. She'd tell him. And when she was finished, he'd probably wish she hadn't. She faced him. "I guess I'm confused. Or conflicted. Or hell, I don't know. I really despised you for so, so long for leaving Mae, for abandoning your kid. These awful things Mae said about you were lodged in my head. And then when Randy dumped Clementine on you, those thoughts and preconceived notions I had about you are...are...*shattered*. I keep trying to pick up the pieces and somehow make sense of it all, but the pieces no longer fit back together, and I'm left with these thoughts in my head that don't jive with what I see every day, from the way you've made Clementine your priority to the gentle way you reprimand her to the loving way you braid her hair when she wants to look like Josephine."

She hadn't noticed the way he'd moved closer as she spoke, the way his hands had gone to her upper arms and slid up and across to her shoulders where his fingers gently kneaded the tired muscles at the base of her neck until it was too late. He didn't say anything, while he waited for her to spit the rest of what she had to say out.

"I guess what I'm trying to say is... You're nothing like I'd expected. And I don't know how to reconcile those two polar-opposite men in my brain."

"I'm not asking you to give me a gold star, but I would appreciate the benefit of the doubt. You don't owe it to me, but I'm asking for it just the same."

She glanced up at him. No matter how good looking or sweet on his daughter he was, she didn't need to get any more tangled up in their lives than she already was. "I want to help. That doesn't make us friends."

"Good."

Did she hear him right? "Good?"

"Yes. Because what I feel can't be labeled as 'friendly.' And neither could that kiss you laid on me."

She stood up straighter. "Clearly, that was a mistake."

His eyes didn't flash with anger. They lit with mischief. He hitched his thumbs in the front pockets of his jeans and rocked back on his heels, his gaze never leaving her face as he appraised her. "Holy hell, Marsh. You're into me."

"Ha," she scoffed because the words not only hit close to home, they landed a direct, obliterating hit. "Like I told you before, I'm not sleeping with you."

"You will." His eyes twinkled in the light as he pushed his cowboy hat farther up his head. "Don't say I didn't warn you."

LEVI TOWELED OFF AND PULLED ON A PAIR OF FRESHLY WASHED AND starched Wranglers from the Lufkin *Fluff and Fold*. He glanced at his watch—an hour or so until Clementine's grandparents showed up for lunch. He'd also bought them tickets to the rodeo later that night, in case they wanted to stay for the fun.

Bam, bam, bam. A fist pounded on his door, the cheap aluminum shaking in the jamb. "Mr. Levi, are you in there?"

He slid his arms into his shirt, his heart picking up an extra beat at the urgency in his babysitter's voice. He pushed the door open. "Sophie, what's wrong?"

The teen's face lacked color, and she stood at his steps, wringing her hands.

At the same time that he asked, "Where's Clementine?" she said, "Is Clementine with you?"

Levi stilled. "What? Why would she be with me? She's supposed to be with you. That's what I'm paying you for."

"I know. I get that. I—I—"

Levi didn't immediately panic. Kids got lost at the rodeo. It was fine. Clementine was fine.

Still, his heart dropped in his chest, and his breakfast considered a repeat appearance. He stomped down the steps as he buttoned his shirt. "What happened?"

"I—We—I mean—I'm so sorry Mr. Levi. I don't know—"

Levi placed his hands on her upper arms and gave them a gentle squeeze. "Sophie, look at me."

When she finally did, her eyes were glossy and rimmed with red. "Take a deep breath and tell me where you were the last time you saw her."

"At the concession stands. She was thirsty, and I didn't want her to have to walk to the water fountains by the rodeo office, so I sat her on one of the picnic tables and went to get her a cup of water. I turned around for a sec—"

That's the information Levi needed. "Go to the rodeo office, have them announce a lost kid. Tell them what she's wearing. I'll go look for her."

"Okay." Tears fell. "I'm so sorry."

Levi tramped down on his anger. At fourteen, Sophie was not much more than a kid herself. She wasn't to blame.

He was.

"It's not your fault. Go on now. Get to the office."

"Yes, sir." Sophie dried her face and took off at a dead run.

Levi jogged through the parking lot and pounded his fist on Josephine's trailer. When she answered, he said, "Clementine's missing from the concession stands. Can you help get the word out?"

"You go," she said, "I'm on it."

Levi had almost made it to the concession stands when

the announcement about Clementine came over the PA system. He called out for his daughter, tamping down on the sense of unease. There were so many places at the rodeo that could be dangerous for little kids. If she'd found her way to the holding pens, she could easily slip into one of the paddocks with the steers, the bucking broncos, or even the bulls.

And he couldn't even think about the chances of a stranger taking her. Though that early in the day, most everyone on the grounds was connected with the rodeo. The crowds wouldn't show up until much later, so the chances of a stranger taking her were much less, but not zero.

As Levi scanned the concession area, Ian came running over. "You find her?"

"No. She couldn't have gone far. Can you check the chutes? I'm headed to the holding pens."

"I'm on it," Ian said as he jogged away. He turned around after a few strides, "Hey, buddy, we're gonna find her."

"Yeah." But as Levi searched under the picnic tables and concession stand trailers and made his way behind the main arena with no sign of his daughter, his apprehension rocketed toward panic.

He ran to the stockyard behind the main arena, his breath coming fast and his heart knocking against his sternum. His boots slipped in the muddy aisle. Lufkin had received much-needed rain in the few days leading up to the rodeo, and the uncovered pens and aisles had become a damn mucky mess.

The animals churned up mud in the pens as they slogged through, their hooves making sucking noises in the muck with each step. Olivia ran toward Levi from the opposite direction.

"I heard," she said, the worry line between her brows digging deep. "I've checked the bullpens. She isn't there."

The constricting band around his chest loosened a fraction

allowing him to breathe a little easier. "Check the bronc pens, I'll check the steer pens."

"I'll meet you at the rear barn entrance."

"See you there."

They split up, and he carefully walked up and down the pens of steers packed so tightly with animals it was nearly impossible to check quickly.

At the last pen, he caught a flash of pink on the far side, covered in mud. It wasn't moving. Without thinking, he hopped the fence, shoving through the filthy animals. He skidded to a stop, going down on one knee near the muddled mess of fabric, digging through the mud with his shaking hands.

No, no, no. God no.

He pulled the object free, turning it over, lifeless eyes opened, a mechanical "momma" whined from an internal speaker. A doll. A *fucking* doll.

Levi hung his head, and took three deep breaths, as the *whoosha, whoosha* of blood roared past his eardrums like water over storm-raged rapids. He stood, the limp doll dangling in his hand.

He wanted to toss it aside, but something inside him wouldn't let him. A steer skittered by, stomping on his boot, and slamming a muck-encrusted rump into his thigh.

He slipped and slid through the pen, almost losing a boot a time or two on the way out. As quickly and thoroughly as he could, he checked the rest of the pens and met Olivia at the back entrance to the barn.

"Anything?" she asked as he walked up.

He glanced down at the doll in his hand and held it up, a strangled chuckle escaped. "I—I found this in one of the pens, I thought—" He cleared his throat, but the emotion dug in its claws and refused to let go.

Olivia's hands went to her face. "Oh, God." She closed the

gap between them and wrapped him in her arms. "That must have been awful," she said, her words muffled as he hugged her tight to his chest.

He didn't say anything, because he couldn't. Seeing the lifeless form of the doll in the mud was the most terrifying moment of his life.

"Clementine! Baby, where are you?" Josephine or Cora called out. From that distance, Levi couldn't tell which.

Olivia took a step back and said, "We're going about this wrong. This place is too big, and there are too many places to hide. Think. If you were her, where would you go if you could go anywhere?"

Levi gathered his thoughts and focused on Olivia's words. If he were Clementine... "Chunk," he said. "She'd find Chunk."

He didn't hesitate, he grabbed her hand, and together they ran through the barn to Chunk's assigned stall. Levi's heart stuttered, and his stomach dropped when he saw his horse's stall door open enough for a curious three-year-old to slip through.

His horse's head wasn't visible through the bars. They slowed a few stalls away from Chunk's. If Chunk was laying down and if his daughter was in the stall with him, he didn't want to rush up to his horse and risk startling him.

Shoving the doll into Olivia's hands, he walked up to the stall entrance, his pace slow and even. He glanced in at his dozing gelding laying on his sternum in a pile of fresh pine shavings in the center of his stall.

In the pocket between Chunk's front and rear legs, lay a sleeping Clementine.

Olivia sucked in a startled breath and whispered. "*Levi...*"

"It's okay," he said into her ear, maybe more to comfort himself than her. "Chunk wouldn't hurt her on purpose."

He placed his hand on the stall door, ready to shove it open if he had to scramble to protect Clementine. "Hey, buddy," he said to Chunk in a low, soothing voice.

Chunk's eyes opened, and he let loose a startled snort. The horse shifted, stretching his front legs more out in front of him as if he were going to stand. "Easy now. *Eaaasy*."

Chunk stilled, then settled back into the shavings with a huge sigh, swinging his big head around and sniffing at the sleeping Clementine. Levi eased the stall door open.

"I'm going to his head in case he tries to get up," Levi said. "You slip in behind me and get Clementine."

"Got it."

Levi stepped in, keeping up a constant, soothing chatter to Chunk full of "easy does its" and "atta boys." He squatted in front of his horse, taking the big head in his hands and putting it over his shoulder, scratching and scrubbing at the spots behind Chunk's ears that his horse loved to have rubbed. Chunk huffed, and his eyes rolled.

"Go ahead," Levi said. "He's not going anywhere."

Olivia stepped in, gathered up Clementine, and stepped out of the stall.

Levi dropped to his knees, patting his horse's neck. "You're a rock star, boy."

When Levi stood, Chunk stretched his front legs in front of him and heaved himself up, shaking the loose shavings from his mane and forelock.

Clementine whined in Olivia's arms as she woke up then welled up with tears. "I wanna sleep whiff Chunky."

"Oh baby," Olivia said, "You can't sleep with the horses."

"But he wuvs me," Clementine wailed, her tears forming fat droplets on her cheeks, her face going a deeper shade of pink than her dress.

Levi tossed a thick flake of alfalfa into Chunk's pen and slid the door closed. He reached for his daughter and said, "He does, Pix, but stalls aren't for little girls to sleep in."

Her breaths came in soft, hitching gasps, the tears still flowing. Olivia picked stray bits of shavings out of her hair. Then Clementine went still, and the crying abruptly stopped as she stared at something over Levi's shoulder.

"Oh," Clementine said, "A baby doll." Then she put her little hands on either side of his face the way she did when she wanted to make sure he was paying extra close attention to what she was about to say. "Is that for me?"

Levi turned, and Clementine scrambled out of his arms. The doll lay in a muddy heap where Olivia had dropped it in front of the next stall over. Clementine squatted down and reached for one of the life-like hands, then stopped. She glanced back up at Levi, her little nose scrunched up. "Why she ucky?"

"I'll get her," Levi said. "You don't want to get your new dress dirty."

He picked up the doll by the one clean spot on her dress. "We'll get her cleaned up, then you can play with her."

"We will?" Olivia and Clementine said at the same time.

Clementine looked thrilled. Olivia looked doubtful and shook her head. She leaned in, whispering in his ear, "She's got you gut-hooked."

Then she stepped back and said, "Is there anything you won't do for that kid?"

Levi chuckled, shaking his head. "Not a da—darn thing."

5

"I STILL SAY THIS IS A BAD IDEA," OLIVIA MUTTERED.

She and Levi sat in her truck in front of a local Lufkin diner with Clementine standing on the seat between them as they waited for Clementine's grandparents to arrive.

"I can't keep them from her."

"You can. You should."

"You said yourself that Randy would leave her with them for a night or two every now and then when he needed a break. I know Mae and her parents didn't get along and I can appreciate the fact that she didn't want our daughter to be raised by them, but seriously, they can't be that bad."

Olivia scoffed but didn't bother saying anything. She had a feeling Levi would find out real soon how wrong he was.

A car pulled up beside them, a black, four-door coupe. The car freshly washed, the windows clean and free of smudges. Everything neat and clean and perfect.

"Is that them?" Levi asked.

"Yeah." Olivia sighed. She really didn't want to be here, but Levi had asked, and a part of her thought that letting him go alone would be like sending the lamb to slaughter. So, she came. Though now she felt more like Judas. "You owe me," she said as she popped the door latch and stepped out of the truck.

Levi climbed out a few seconds later with Clementine in his arms. Olivia came around the front of the truck as the Jordan's locked and closed their doors.

"Hello, again." Olivia stood back and gave them a little wave. Even if she'd wanted to give them a hug, they weren't the kind of people who welcomed it.

"Olivia."

How one simple flat word could hold so much disdain, Olivia didn't know. Maybe it wasn't her aunt's tone so much as the way the woman looked her up and down from the scuff on Olivia's work boots to the men's style shirt she wore. Olivia had packed for the rodeo ready to work, not to socialize.

Levi glanced from Mae's mother to Olivia, as if unsure what to say. Even Clementine was unusually quiet. Then Levi shifted Clementine to his hip and stuck out his hand to Mae's father. "Levi Banks, pleased to meet you, sir."

"Clive Jordan," Mae's father shook his hand after a beat. "My wife, June."

Levi tipped his hat. "Ma'am."

June *harrumphed*, and her lips got pinched and puckered liked she'd sucked the ever-loving life out of a lemon.

"Clementine," Levi said, "Say hello to your grandma and grandpa."

Instead of her usual boisterous hello, Clementine snuggled against Levi's neck and muttered a soft, "Hi."

The five of them stood there. Clive in his baby-blue seersucker suit, June in her yellow double-knit polyester, white-gloved hands clutching her matching handbag in front of her. They looked like they belonged back in the fifties, not here in the seventies.

"After you," Levi said, his arm outstretched motioning Olivia and the Jordans ahead of him.

In the diner, the waitress ushered them into a red vinyl booth. Olivia slid in first with Levi sitting next to her. They put Clementine at the end of the table in a booster seat the waitress brought. Clive ended up across from Olivia and June sat across from Levi, so she could be closer to Clementine.

They looked at the menus in silence and placed their orders when the waitress came back by and dropped off three crayons and a color sheet for Clementine.

"That's a lot of food for one little girl," June said as the waitress took their menus and stepped away. "No wonder she's looking so plump."

Olivia had to swallow the '*are you freaking kidding me?*' The words slid back down her throat like rusty razors.

Levi stilled, then sat up straighter and in a voice that seemed much more reasonable than the comment deserved said, "The pediatrician said she's still below the curve on weight and height. Besides, she doesn't have to eat everything now. I can take the leftovers back to the camper for later."

"A camper." June's face soured again. "Is that really a proper place for a little girl to live?"

Before Levi could defend himself, Clive jumped in. "A man, a *real* father, should want the best for his child. Not a camper in a parking lot."

Levi turned his attention to Clive, the tick at the corner of his jaw the only indication of his annoyance.

"Clementine has a roof over her head, food in her belly, and people who love her unconditionally. *That's* what's best for *my* child."

Olivia cocked her head, seeing a side of Levi she hadn't seen before. Though from what she'd learned about him, his view as his role as a father shouldn't have floored her. Levi didn't have a lot, yet Clementine didn't want for anything. To a man like Levi, amassing material possessions wasn't his top priority.

A chill settled over the table. June glanced over at Clementine who was busy coloring a horse a dark red, her squiggly lines obliterating the shape of the horse.

"Oh, no, dear." June took the crayon out of Clementine's hands. "You color inside the lines."

June carefully colored a bale of hay, making sure no marks went astray. She handed the crayon back to Clementine who picked another color and started coloring the truck, turning it into a big blob of blue.

"Baby. You're doing it wrong." June snatched the crayon out of Clementine's hands.

Clementine's smile fell, her lips got pouty, and her sweet blue eyes rimmed with red.

"Leave her be, June," Levi said, his voice deceptively calm.

June met Levi's level gaze and handed the crayon back.

"June's right," Clive chimed in. "How's the child going to learn if you don't show her how to color correctly?"

Levi's back went rigid, and Olivia's hand went to his thigh and gave him a supportive squeeze. This was what she'd warned him about. The incessant picking, the toxic nagging, the scalding judgment. He covered her hand with his, and gave it a light squeeze back, relaxing a fraction when he said, "She's three, Clive. She can color however the hell she wants."

"Hell, hell," Clementine said, the smile back on her face.

June clutched at the strand of pearls around her neck, sucking in a scandalized breath. "Well, I never."

"Pix," Levi said in his ever-patient tone. "That's not a nice word."

The waitress came back with her tray loaded down with food before Clementine could say 'hell' another five times and give her grandmother angina. Shame.

They tucked into their food in silence except for the clink of glassware on the table and the squeak of knives across the plates. For a Friday, the lunch crowd was spread thin. The bell on the front door banged and clanked against the glass, and Dusty Wills and a few fellow bulldoggers strode in.

The men found a seat, but Dusty caught Levi's eye and came over, clapping him on the back. "Afternoon, everybody," Dusty said with a tip of his hat. Then to Levi said, "I see you found your kid."

Shit. Olivia needed to shut him down. Fast. "Hey, Dusty, thanks for stopping by, but we're here with family and—"

"What is he talking about, Banks?" Clive asked.

"You didn't hear?" Dusty pulled the toothpick out of his mouth. "Lost the kid this morning. Everyone was looking everywhere."

"*Dusty*," Olivia said, "Do you mind?"

The congenial smile slipped from his face, utterly ignorant of the shit storm about to go down. "Yeah, sure. Sorry." Dusty tipped his hat, but the damage was already done. "Catch you folks later."

"You lost Clementine?" June asked.

"It wasn't like that," Levi tucked his bite of food into his cheek. "She got away from her babysitter and—"

"She could have been trampled by a horse." June's hand once again clasped her pearls like a shield.

Under the table, Levi reached for Olivia's hand. Their fingers linked, and Levi's grip went tight.

"Or a crazy person could have taken her," Clive added for good measure.

"It wasn't the babysitter's fault, she's just a kid—" Levi cut himself off. He must have realized his mistake as soon as the words left his mouth.

"How old was she?" June asked.

"Fourteen," Olivia said, "but she's mature for her age."

"How could you be so irresponsible?" June looked at Levi as if he'd left Clementine with an ax-murderer.

Olivia squeezed his hand. He didn't squeeze back. A blood vessel at his temple throbbed, and red crept past the collar on his shirt.

When Levi didn't answer, June continued, "I will not have my granddaughter—"

"*Enough.*" Levi spat the word through gritted teeth as he slammed his open hand on the table. Plates jumped. A fork clattered to the floor. June's eyes went wide. Clive turned the same shade of red as the vinyl benches, and Clementine screwed up her face and cried.

"Now look what you've done," June said.

"It's okay, Pix." Levi stood and took Clementine out of the booster seat. "I didn't mean to shout."

June leaned across the table toward Olivia and in a harsh whisper, said, "Is he always this angry and out of control?"

Olivia couldn't help the bubble of laughter. "You're kidding me, right?"

But by the contemptuous look on June's face, she wasn't in the least bit kidding.

"You coming?" Levi asked Olivia.

Olivia slid out of the booth. "Definitely."

Clementine burrowed her face into Levi's neck, and he brushed a tear off her cheek. Then he pulled his wallet out of his pocket and tossed down a wad of cash on the table.

"Sit back down, son," Clive said as if his age gave him authority. "Lunch isn't over."

"No, we're definitely done here." Levi started to walk away, then he stopped and tossed two rodeo tickets on top of the cash. To a stunned Clive and June, he said, "The events start at seven.

Clementine's been looking forward to going with you. For her sake, I hope you come."

———

LEVI SETTLED INTO THE BACK OF THE BOX, FEELING MILDLY anxious and out of sorts. Not about his upcoming run, but about the fact that Clementine's grandparents had shown up at the rodeo.

Which had almost worried him more than the idea of finding another babysitter for Clementine for the night. One thing was for certain, something had to give. He couldn't keep passing his kid around to his friends at the rodeo like a hot potato when he had to compete. But clearly, hiring what babysitters he could find hadn't worked out for him either.

He heard a piercing whistle, and Cooter caught his eye from the box on the other side of the steer. "Ready?"

Levi bobbed his head, and the man running the chute released the steer. As soon as he touched his heels to Chunk's sides, his horse jetted off, the steer breaking the barrier a millisecond before Chunk. The spectators in the stands roared as Chunk closed in on the steer, Cooter keeping the animal running straight and true.

Levi leaned out of the saddle and dropped into the hole, inches away from dropping onto the steer when he felt a stutter in Chunk's step. His gelding stumbled and went down in the front, Levi's unbalanced weight and their momentum sending them rolling.

The next few seconds went by in a blur. A hush went through the crowd. Levi hit the ground, managing to cover his head in time as Chunk crashed down around him. He took a hit to his leg and chest, then opened his eyes only to see Chunk's rear hoof coming down.

Levi rolled, the edge of Chunk's hoof thumped the side of his head. Pain skittered around his skull, his ears buzzed, and his vision went wonky, and then his world went black.

When he woke, he still lay in the arena, a firm hand held on his shoulder when he went to roll on his hands and knees.

"Stay still," Cooter said. "Let them ambulance guys check ya out."

Levi settled back into the dirt because it hurt his head too much to move. "How's Chunk?"

"Trotted off sound. Don't worry 'bout him none. I'll take care of him. Worry about yourself."

The pounding in his head eased, and his vision began to clear. Again, Levi rolled onto his hands and knees, and this time Cooter let him.

"Easy now," Cooter said as he helped Levi to his feet.

The crowd cheered, and Levi raised a shaky hand to the fans. He swayed and a paramedic running into the arena caught him.

"You need to sit down," the man said. Levi looked again. Not a man. Not much more than a baby-faced kid.

Levi steadied himself and shook off the helping hand. "I'm fine. Give me a sec."

Something warm dribbled down the side of his face. He reached up, and his fingers came away covered in blood.

"Here." The paramedic came up with a handful of gauze squares. "Hold this on there until we can get a better look at it."

Levi sucked in a breath as the paramedic slapped the gauze onto the wound, but he held it tight to his head. Though he didn't need it, the paramedic kept a strong hand wrapped around Levi's bicep as he limped out of the arena.

"The leg bad, too?" the paramedic asked.

Levi didn't stop walking to work his leg, the pain and the limp already diminishing as he kept moving. "Bruised. Not broken."

The ambulance had been moved to the alley behind the arena, so he didn't have far to walk. With a little help, he climbed into the ambulance and sat heavily on the gurney.

The paramedic laid him down, palpating his abdomen for indications of pain and possible internal injuries, then started taking his blood pressure and checking his eyes with a little light that made his head pound even harder.

Olivia walked up to the open rear door of the ambulance. "Hey, you okay?" Her voice wasn't strained, there wasn't any trace of distress in her voice.

He knew how bad these things could look from the stands. He appreciated the fact Olivia wasn't the type of person who got hysterical.

"I'm good." Levi sat up with a grunt. "A few bruises and a bump on the head. Nothing major. Right, Doc?"

The paramedic made him follow the movement of the retina-melting penlight, then clicked it off—*thank God.*

With what sounded like reluctance, the kid agreed. "You'll live."

"Oh, shit," Olivia said.

Levi chuckled. "I didn't think you'd take the news of me surviving so hard."

"Not that." Olivia tossed her head toward the threesome approaching them. "It's Clementine and the Jordans."

Levi's pulse kicked up, doubling the pain and throbbing in his head. "Oh, shit's right."

The paramedic dabbed at his head wound with a wad of gauze soaked in disinfectant. Levi bit back the string of curse words he wanted to let fly as Clive, June, and Clementine walked up.

"Lebi!" Clementine called out.

"How ya doin', Pix?"

She squirmed in June's arms until she had to be put down.

Olivia helped Clementine into the ambulance.

She climbed onto the gurney. "Why you bweeding?"

"It's just a scratch," Levi said. "Nothing to worry about."

"Nothing to worry about?" June's voice had gone shrill. If there had been any coyotes around, they would have started howling. "You could have been killed."

"*June.*" Levi bobbed his chin toward Clementine. "Now's not the time."

"Have you thought about what would happen to your daughter if you were maimed or k—"

Levi cut her off with a look. "I'm extremely good at what I do. I'm not going to get hurt."

"You're already hurt, son." Levi didn't need Clive jumping down his throat as well.

"It's just a few lumps and bumps. I'm good to go, right?" Levi tried pulling the paramedic into the conversation.

The man glanced at the dyspeptic expression on June's face. "Ah—he—he doesn't even need stitches."

"See? All I need is a Band-Aid and I'm good to go."

"I didn't say that."

"Work with me, man," Levi muttered under his breath.

"What do you mean, young man?" June planted her white-gloved hands on her yellow covered hips.

The paramedic gave Levi one of those half-grimace, half-smiles that said don't-put-me-in-the-middle. Levi was big enough to break this guy over his knee, yet the kid was more worried about a hundred pounds of pissed-off housewife.

"I'm saying he's had a hard knock to the head. He should at least go to the hospital and get—"

"No hospital." Levi couldn't afford a damn trip to the hospital. Especially now that he had another mouth to feed. Besides, he'd taken hits to the head a lot harder than that one. His vision was clear. The pain in his head he could tolerate, and he refused to give June and Clive more ammunition against him.

The paramedic cleaned up the blood from the side of his face the best he could. "Then you need to take it easy for the next few days. Drink lots of fluids, get a lot of rest."

Easy for the paramedic to say. He looked barely old enough to shave. Levi doubted he had a clue what life was like as a single father to a rambunctious three-year-old.

"Done," Levi lied. He didn't have the time to laze around doing nothing, though it wouldn't do any good to argue.

"We're taking Clementine," June said.

"What?" Levi and Olivia said at the same time. His world tilted for a second when he whipped his head around, and the pounding reached a level where it almost became impossible to hide his grimace.

"For the night," June added. "We'll bring her back before lunch tomorrow."

As much as he didn't want Clementine to go with Mae's parents, the pounding in his head told him he probably wouldn't be worth shit tonight. He glanced at Olivia.

She shrugged one shoulder and said, "It's probably not a bad idea."

Then he took his daughter's hand in his, and said in the most positive, most cajoling voice he could drum up, "What do you think, Pix? You wanna have a sleepover with your grandma and grandpa tonight?"

Her smile went wide, and she batted those innocent blue eyes at him. When she got close to dating age, he was gonna need a big-ass shotgun.

"Sweepober!" She hopped off the gurney and danced around in the tight space. "I'm gonna hab a sweepober."

Her reaction came as a surprise to him, but maybe Clive and June were only intolerable when adults were around. She'd already spent several hours with her grandparents and seemed perfectly content to spend even more time with them.

He locked eyes with Clive. "I'll pick her up at seven in the morning. She likes to feed Chunk."

Then to the paramedic, he said, "We about done here?"

"I need to put a bandage on, and you're good to go."

"Give me a minute," he said to Clive and June, "and I'll get her pajamas and a change of clothes."

Olivia patted him on the knee, her hand lingering a beat longer than it should. "Stay put. I'll take care of it."

Levi dug his keys out of his pocket—his dick reading much more into the touch than the situation warranted—and tossed them to her. "Thanks."

He hugged and kissed Clementine goodnight, and Clive gave him the name of the motel and the number of the room where they were staying. Then he watched the four of them walk away.

"Your girl's beautiful," the paramedic said as he placed the clean gauze square over the butterfly bandages and wound the roll of bandage material around and around his head.

"She's a great kid."

Color infused the paramedic's cheeks. "I wasn't talking about the kid."

Levi opened his mouth to tell the guy that Olivia wasn't his, but, "I'm lucky to have her in my life," came tumbling out.

It wasn't the full truth. But it also wasn't a damn lie.

"You didn't have to wait." Levi's voice came out of the dark moments before Olivia saw his form. He moved slow and had a mild limp, carrying his mangled hat in his hand.

She stood up from his camper step and held out his keys. "I wanted to wait so I could give your keys back."

He tossed them through the open door onto Clementine's bed. "You could have left them inside. No one would have bothered my stuff. I don't even know why I bother locking it."

She shrugged. It wasn't about locking up. It was about making sure he was really as okay as he tried to make everyone believe. She'd seen wicked wrecks before, and he'd been lucky to come away without any major damage. "Is Chunk okay?"

"Looked like it. Cooter stopped by the ambulance with him. He didn't look lame. I'll throw him in the round pen in the morning and make sure he's still sound."

"You got lucky."

"I'm good at dodging bullets."

"As much as I hate to say this, June wasn't entirely off base." When his eyes narrowed at her, she quickly added, "About you getting hurt, I mean. Have you thought about what would happen to Clementine if—?" She cut herself off. Not wanting to say the words *if you died* out loud. As if speaking it would make it so. She reached up and touched the bandage wrapped around his head. The last thing Clementine needed was to be an orphan.

That's it? All you're worried about is how Clementine would feel?

The kid had been through a lot already, losing her mother—

Admit it, your worry about him isn't only for Clementine's sake, it's for your sake as well. You like him, Olivia. Admit it.

As in like *like.*

As in your feelings are more than platonic.

As in you'd like to take your hands and—

"Fine. I admit it."

Levi reached up and took her hand in his, with a light chuckle. "You admit what?"

She squeezed her eyes and shook her head before looking back up at him. His eyes were bright and that crooked, sexy smile, beamed back at her. "Nothing. It's been a long day and an even longer night."

"It's not even that late."

"Feels like it."

He still had her hand, his thumb bumping back and forth across her knuckles, raising goosebumps on her arms. He leaned against his camper, forcing her to take a step closer. Then she took another on her own. "Are you really okay?"

He brought her hand to his lips and planted a kiss on the palm of her hand. "I'm better now."

He tugged her in between his legs, and she went willingly. Tucking their joined hands to his chest, he cupped her cheek, his thumb brushing across her bottom lip. His gaze flicked down when she ran her tongue over the pad of his thumb.

His eyes went dark, and he dipped his head. "I'm going to kiss you, Olivia Marsh."

"I think you should." Her answer came out no more than a whisper.

He touched his lips to hers, then pulled away a fraction, and she had to bite back the groan of frustration. "You do?" He sounded taken aback, as if what she'd said finally registered.

"I do." She slid her hand behind his neck and pulled him back into the kiss.

He opened her mouth with his, and her tongue met him halfway. That close, she smelled disinfectant on his skin. Her stomach did a tiny flip when her brain went to that terrible place that gamed out every possible tragic thing that could have happened to him. If he only knew how hard it had been for her to keep her shit together when she'd approached the ambulance.

He pulled back and said, "Hey, you still with me here?"

Smooth, Marsh. She touched her head to his chest, then looked back up at the concern on his face. "I'm here."

"Where'd you go?"

"Someplace I don't want to be."

He studied her. His fingers tracing across her forehead, down her temples to her cheekbones, then he cupped her face in his large, calloused hands.

Ducking his head again, he drew her into the kiss, the light exploratory touch of their lips quickly turning deep and demanding. She angled her head and raised up on her toes, taking the kiss even deeper.

His hands started roaming, and she arched into him. It took everything she had not to take his hands and slap them on her breasts or her ass or the V between her legs.

She shifted and straddled his thick thigh, his arousal pressing into her hip. He broke the kiss, and they both struggled to catch their breath. He nipped down her neck, his hands cupping her ass and pulling her in tighter. She ground against him, and he groaned.

Into her ears, he said, "I like you here."

She ran her hand down his chest to the bump of muscles across his abdomen. "In your arms?"

"In my life."

In my life. He must have rattled a few brain cells to have said that, but a little thump on the head wouldn't stop her. Her hand went lower and lower until she cupped him through his jeans.

He hissed in a breath, his head falling back, thumping against the camper. "Jesus Christ, woman."

"You like?" she asked as she continued to fondle him, loving how his breath had gone ragged and he'd grown impossibly harder under her touch.

"You know I do."

With her other hand, she popped the top two snaps on his western shirt and buried her face in his chest and started kissing her way across the wide expanse of hard muscle.

"You realize we're out in the open here, right?" Though that didn't keep him from running his hands up her sides and his thumbs from skimming the underside of her breasts.

"That big rig is blocking everyone's view." She ran her fingernail up his zipper. That far out in the parking lot, it was quiet, and she could hear her nail drag along the zipper teeth until she reached his belt buckle. They really should take things inside, but she couldn't wait that long to get her hands, her tongue, her lips, on him.

She unfastened the large silver and gold championship buckle he'd won the year before and had reached for the button on his jeans when one of his large hands came down on hers.

"What are we doing, Liv?"

Liv. In the past, she'd admonished him when he'd called her that, but now... now so many things had changed. That word, that familiarity that had grated her nerves now made the blood whoosh behind her ears. "If I have to explain it to you..." she teased.

She tried to shake off his hand, but he held on tighter.

He took in a deep breath and blew it out. "Maybe this isn't such a good idea."

"You're kidding me, right?" Though even before he answered, she knew he wasn't. It was written on his face—in the lines on his forehead, in the tension around his eyes.

His breathing slowed, and the heat, the passion that had been there seconds before, cleared away. "Look. My life's pretty complicated right now."

Yeah. And she was one more complication he didn't need. She lifted her hands in surrender. "It's okay. I get it."

She patted him on the chest. "I'm going back to the ranch after this rodeo anyway. It would be stupid... you know... you and me..."

"It's not stupid, it's—"

"It's okay." She didn't bother hiding her disappointment. She wasn't into head games. It was what it was, and she wasn't going to pretend to feel anything that she didn't.

"I'm really sorry," he said as he refastened his belt buckle.

"Don't be." She took another step back. Not embarrassed or angry but confused and in truth, a little hurt. He'd seemed as into her as she'd been into him. She turned to go. "Night."

His hand came down on her wrist, locking her in place. "Why didn't you tell me you were leaving?"

"You knew this was a temporary gig until Rusty got up to speed and I could take his training wheels off."

"You still could have said something sooner."

"Then I guess we've both been a little caught off guard."

"This isn't what I want." The sincerity in his tone rang true.

She pulled her arm free, and he let her go. "Me neither."

6

AFTER WATCHING OLIVIA DRIVE AWAY, LEVI STOMPED UP THE STEPS of his camper, not sure which head hurt the most, the big one or the little one.

He reached into the cabinet above the stove and poured a healthy dose of analgesics into his hand and washed it down with a fresh beer out of his refrigerator. At least he had an easy solution for one of his problems.

If only his remedy for Olivia were that simple.

He set the beer down, his full bladder nagging him, but he could only stand there at his toilet with his hard-on in his hand, trying to take a piss. He thought long and hard about rubbing one out, but he didn't want his hand, he wanted Olivia.

He leaned an arm against the upper cabinet and waited, his gaze dropping to the mud-caked doll Olivia had left in his shower pan. When he finally finished, he washed his hands and picked up the doll.

One inanimate eye opened. The other remained closed and dirt clogged, the "momma" sounding hollow and creepy in the confines of the camper. Maybe he should toss the doll and get

73

Clementine something new, but that wasn't what he'd promised her.

Since Clementine was gone for the night, he converted her bed back into the table and settee. He had to come up with a better living solution if he and Clementine were going to stay on the road together. But that worry was for another day.

He set the doll on the seat closest to the stove and took a quick shower to wash the arena dirt and disinfectant off him. When he'd finished, he threw on a pair of sweats and removed the damp bandage from around his head and examined the damage in the bathroom mirror. The bruising and swelling were surprisingly minimal. The cut ran deep, but the butterfly bandages kept the edges closed.

He'd gotten lucky. Dodged a bullet, like he'd told Olivia.

One of these days, you'll be too slow, too pre-occupied, too old, too something *and that bullet will hit. This is rodeo. It's not a matter of* if *but* when.

He stepped away from the mirror, unable to look himself in the face. He had difficult decisions to make for his sake as well as Clementine's.

Grabbing his beer, he sat with his back to the door, his bare feet propped up on the seat across from him. He stared at the doll. She stared back. Her dark hair lay matted against her plastic skull, mud caking her face like a kind of skin care mask, that one eye winking at him as if they shared an inside joke.

Only he wasn't laughing.

If Clementine were with him, he'd be cooking her dinner, or helping her with her shower, or maybe they'd be tucked up in his bed reading one of her picture books on farm animals.

But she wasn't there, and the camper was too quiet. His *life* was too quiet. What the hell had he done with his nights before?

Had he always been this damn lonely?

He took another swig of beer and rested his head against the wall, closing his eyes. The beer and the analgesics would beat the throbbing in his head down to the occasional dull thud if he didn't move too quickly.

He waited for his thoughts to settle, for the sleep to creep in, but his mind ping-ponged between Clementine and Olivia. Between trying to do what's right for both of the women in his life and not lose himself in the process. He'd been right not to take things any further with Olivia. It didn't matter that they both wanted the same thing in the moment. She was leaving and—

You didn't know that when you stopped her from putting her hands on you.

Didn't matter. She was leaving. He was a father with new responsibilities and commitments and—

Desires.

Damn.

He opened his eyes and stared down at the doll. "Why can't I get them out of my head?"

Dolly didn't have any answers or words of wisdom. She just sat there, dropping bits of dried dirt onto the seat.

He set the beer down. He couldn't sit there talking to a damn doll all evening. With a groan, he slid out of the seat. "Time to get you more presentable."

Over the next half hour, he stripped the doll and hand-washed her clothes in the sink and hung them to dry on the clothesline strung across his bathroom. Then he took one of Chunk's old snaggle-toothed tail brushes and washed and brushed the doll's hair until the tangles cleared and mud swirled down the sink. Then he took a damp washcloth to the body, careful not to get the internal speaker wet.

The whole time his mind kept returning to Olivia's question—What if something happened to him? What if? What if?

Was he making a colossal mistake? Should he do right by

Clementine and let her grandparents raise her in a home where she could have friends and school and *stability*?

Damned if he knew.

But he did know that giving her up wouldn't be easy.

———

Olivia laid on the lumpy bed in the cheap motel on the outskirts of Lufkin, listening to the soft *tic, tic, tic* of her windup alarm clock on the bedside table as she watched the second-hand sweep around the dial again.

Her stomach grumbled but she couldn't drum up the energy to get back in her truck and pick something up from the diner. She thought about working on the list of duties, contact numbers, and whatever else she could think of to give to Rusty when she left him in charge of the road stock, but she'd already tried, and what she'd ended up with was a bunch of silly doodles in her notebook.

She'd thought when the day came to return to the ranch, she'd be kicking up her heels and waving *adios* and good riddance, but as much as she hated the impermanence of life on the road, there had been one bright constant—Levi and Clementine.

For once, she had a good reason to stay on the road but even if she'd wanted to, she knew she couldn't. Her grandfather was running the ranch while she'd been gone. He hadn't complained. He loved the life as much as she did, but his health wasn't what it used to be. The long hard days had taken their toll on a man beaten down by wear and tear and age.

She couldn't risk him working himself so hard that he ended up back in the hospital.

There came a knock on the door, and Olivia glanced at the clock. It was only a little after ten at night. Rusty had her number at the motel. If there had been a problem with any of the stock, he could have called her from one of the pay phones, not shown up at her door.

"Who is it?" She rolled off the bed and shoved her legs into a pair of jeans, letting the long hem of her over-sized Waylon Jennings concert T-shirt cover her open fly.

"It's me," Levi said from the other side of the door.

She hurried over, removing the chain, and opening the door. "Is everything okay? Clementine—"

"She's fine. At least as far as I know." He stood there, one large hand gripping the jamb above the door. He was dressed in a ratty T-shirt and an old pair of sweats, looking freshly showered but completely done in.

She leaned against the edge of the open door. Why was he here?

Before she could speak, he asked, "What am I doing?"

He could mean any number of things. What was he doing bringing her dinner, since he had a bag of takeout in his hand that smelled amazing? He could have meant what was he doing coming to her door late at night, or what was he doing when he'd turned her down for sex.

But by that haunted look on his face, she knew he had to be referring to Clementine.

"You wanna come in?"

He nodded.

Plucking the dangling bag from his fingers, she stepped back and let him in. They settled at the table under the window, where the ancient air conditioner spit out fractionally cooler air every once in a while. She pulled out cartons of food.

"Which do you want? The lasagna or the chicken fried steak and mashed potatoes?"

"Lady's choice."

She picked the lasagna and passed out the plastic ware.

Aiming her fork at his forehead, she asked, "Where's the bandage?"

He swallowed a bite of potatoes. "Got damp in the shower. I really don't need it. The head wrap was a bit of an overkill."

"I guess you've got to give the paramedic points for enthusiasm."

Levi mumbled something around a bite of food that sounded like an agreement.

"But that wasn't what you wanted to talk about, was it?"

His swallowed and wiped his mouth. "It's not."

"Then what is it?"

Glancing down at his partially eaten meal, he pushed his plate away as if his stomach had gone sour. "You got anything to drink?"

"Beer." She bumped her chin toward a small cooler by the dresser. "Grab me one, too."

Levi popped the tops off the bottles of beer using the edge of the table and handed one to Olivia. She tucked her heels on the seat and rested her chin on her knees.

He took several long pulls of his beer, swirling the bottle through the drops of water dripping from the bottom. "More than anything, I want to make sure I do right by my girl."

He met her eyes, and every raw emotion he had for Clementine shined in his eyes. Commitment. Protection. Pride. Love. Devotion. For that brief moment, he let her see everything that he was, everything he felt.

Her chest went tight, and her throat felt like a tumbleweed had lodged itself halfway down. Unable to speak, she waited him out.

"I'd be lying if I said this was how I'd pictured my life, a single father trying to make a living on the circuit dragging his kid from one arena to the next. It's a difficult, demanding life for an adult. It can't be easy for a kid."

Olivia took a swallow of beer to clear her throat, though her words still came out raspy. "You love her. That's what matters."

Levi scoffed, shaking his head, and draining the last of his beer. "Is it? She sleeps on a damn table. She doesn't have a yard to run in, or friends her own age to play with. And what about school? What then? How am I—"

"Take it." She handed him her beer. He needed it much more than she did. In a few slugs, he drained that one as well.

He wiped his mouth with the back of his hand. "How am I going to give her everything she needs? How am I going to keep her safe? You saw what happened out there today." His voice broke, but he didn't let that stop him. "What if it hadn't been a doll in that steer pen? What if that had been Clementine? I can't lose her. Not now."

"All you can do is your best."

He buried his face in his hands, his fingers raking through his hair. Then he looked back up at her, his eyes almost empty. "It's not good enough. Not for her."

She stood and went to him, taking his hands and wrapping them around her waist. He rested his chin on her abdomen as he stared up at her.

With her hands cupping his face she said, "What happened this morning happens to every parent. Maybe not at the rodeo, but at a store, or the park, or a busy street. It happens. As for the yard, she has whole rodeo grounds to run around in and explore. Kids in every city she stays in to play with. And school... school is at least two years away. That's not something you have to worry about right now."

She ran her hands through his hair, careful to avoid his injury. "All I know is Clementine is happier and healthier than I've ever seen her. No one has been able to give her that. Only you."

He sat up a little straighter, tugging her closer. "Maybe."

"Don't worry. We'll figure this out."

For the first time since he came over, the tension in his expression eased, and one corner of his mouth turned up in a grin. "We?"

She gave him a shrug and one of those what-can-I-say smiles. Levi Banks had a way of winning a girl over. If anyone doubted his powers, just look at Clementine. "She's my blood, too. As much as I can be in her life, as much as you will allow me, I want to be. I've already lost Mae. I don't want to lose Clementine, too."

He wrapped his arms tighter around her and pressed a kiss to the middle of her abdomen, then glanced up at her. "I'd like that."

Then his eyes shifted from something that resembled appreciation to something much more mischievous and lascivious. He ran his hands down to the hem of her shirt and back up again until he hit bare skin. The muscles in her abdomen quaked under his featherlight touch. "There's something else I'd like as well."

The thought of turning him down never crossed her mind, but she couldn't let his earlier rejection go without at least giving him a good-natured ribbing. "What about your life being 'complicated'?"

"Forgive me," he said, as he raised her shirt above her waist and kissed the skin south of her belly button. "I wasn't thinking straight."

She laughed. "Oh, and now you are thinking clearly after guzzling two beers in as many minutes?"

"It takes more than a couple beers to get me buzzed." He wrapped his arms around the tops of her thighs and stood with her in his arms, his face at chest level. Her nipples peaked, pressing against the thin blue cotton.

"*Sweet baby Jesus.* You're not wearing a bra."

He turned his head, nipping at her through the fabric. It took everything not to wrap her arms around his head and keep him there. "You going to put me down?"

He stepped over to the bed. "If you insist."

Then he dropped her on her back in the middle of the mattress. She laughed as she bounced. Levi landed beside her. He stretched out, his large hand spanning across her abdomen, his thumb drawing loose circles above her hip bone.

He leaned in, taking her mouth with his with a hesitancy that hadn't been there before. He drew a finger down her jaw line. "You good with this?"

She ran her hand over the bulge of his bicep. "Yeah."

"Sorry about earlier. I was an idiot."

"Yes. You were."

He laughed. The deep rumble settled around her, wreaking havoc on her nerves. "Do you always say exactly what's on your mind?"

"I could stop."

By the grin on his face, they both knew it wasn't the truth. "Don't you dare."

But Olivia wasn't finished. When he leaned in to kiss her again, she laid a staying hand on his chest. There was one last thing she needed to clear up. "What about Cora?"

"She's with Ian." When it became clear things weren't going any further until he elaborated, he said, "Look, it's no secret I was sweet on her. We had good times. Great times, even."

"I don't have a problem with you being her friend or cherishing the good memories that you two shared. I'm just saying I don't want to be the runner-up at the county fair. I don't want the red ribbon."

"I'm not going to lie. There had been a while there—until more recently than I'd like to admit—that if she'd wanted me back, I would have said yes. Which would have been a mistake.

She's still a great friend. I want Cora in my life, but I have no desire to have her in my bed."

"Is that the I-will-take-what-I-can-get libido talking?"

"No. That's me."

A month ago, she probably would have called bullshit on that, but in that time, he'd been honest and true. He was a man who lived up to his responsibilities. A man who lived with integrity.

She took his words at face value. "That's what I needed to know."

That time when he kissed her, he didn't hesitate to take the kiss deeper. She opened to him, tasting the beer on his tongue and smelling the soap on his skin. His hand on her abdomen slipped lower, his pinkie dipping beneath the waistband of her jeans and panties.

He broke the kiss and said, "Your jeans are undone."

"I know."

A low growl sent goosebumps down her sides and heat to her core. If he didn't get inside her quick—

Her hand went to his before he could go any farther. "Please tell me you brought a condom."

Grinning, he reached his hand to his back pocket. Then his face fell, and he stood, patting the front and back of his sweats. "Shit. I must have left my wallet in my jeans. Any chance you—"

He didn't even have a chance to get the sentence out before she was shaking her head. "I hadn't planned on having sex while on the road, so..." She raised up on her elbows. "I guess this means this is a no go."

He straddled her hips. She stopped him with a hand on his chest. "What are you doing, we can't—"

He kissed her to shut her up, making her head spin and her breathing accelerate. "There are many things we can do that don't include fucking."

Fucking. None of the men she'd been with before had talked to her that way. It should have turned her off but like a breath of air, it stoked the fire, revved her engines, and made her wheels spin out of control.

"Like what?" she asked, not because she was clueless, but because she wanted to hear him say it out loud.

He chuckled. "Oh, baby, aren't you naughty?" He shifted between her legs, hooking his fingers into the waistband of her jeans and tugging them down. "I'm going to start with my mouth on you." He stopped the slow slide of her pants down her thighs long enough to cup her. She arched up, grinding against his hand. "And we'll work our way down from there."

Slowly, Levi dragged Olivia's jeans down her long legs, enjoying the rash of goosebumps that broke out over her skin as he trailed a lagging finger down each leg.

She was still lying on her back, propped up on her elbows watching his every move. At the foot of the bed, he dropped her jeans and quickly stripped off his own clothes.

"Oh, Lord." Her gaze dropped, and the avid longing in her eyes made him impossibly hard, insanely ravenous. "Bring that baby up here where I can get my hands on you."

"Patience."

"I'm fresh out."

"Too bad," he said as he climbed back onto the mattress between her legs. Her eyes narrowed, but her playful grin told him her devious mind was already calculating tortuous, mind-blowing ways of paying him back. He looked forward to that. "Take off the T-shirt."

He didn't have to ask twice. She laid back down, fully

exposed. Breast wise, she lacked Cora's size and volume, but what she possessed, he found infinitely more attractive.

Confidence.

Confidence that what she had was enough.

Confidence that *she* was enough.

Of the women he'd been with, she was the first woman who hadn't covered her breasts the first time she bared them to him. She traced a lazy finger down her sternum. His eyes locked onto the movement as he followed her finger across the gentle rise of one breast as it skipped across a taut peak.

He had more immediate plans, but that finger...

He dropped down on his forearms and nestled between her thighs, trapping his erection between their bodies as he laved her nipple and sucked it into his mouth. She groaned. Her back arched. Her pelvis ground against him. Levi wanted nothing more than to shift and bury himself balls deep in her warm, wet, walls, but that wasn't going to happen. Not this time.

But until then, he'd make damn sure they both enjoyed themselves enough that there'd *be* a next time. She encircled her arms around his head and held him in place, the sounds escaping the back of her throat made his balls buzz.

He released her, his mouth making a soft *pop* as he worked his way to the other side. He couldn't be partial. He loved her responsiveness, the way her hands tangled in his hair, the way her short fingernails scratched and clawed at his shoulder, the way her ankles locked, and her heels pressed against his hamstrings urging him closer.

He kissed his way up her chest, his tongue dipping into the divot between her collarbones. "I love the way you taste. Fresh like the first cut of summer hay, salty like a woman unafraid of hard work."

She pulled him up, mashing her mouth against his, and he

savored the sweet, sharp sting of her teeth on his bottom lip before a swipe of her tongue soothed the soreness away.

"Don't forget your promise." The way her voiced dipped low with need had him remapping his trajectory.

"I'm on it, boss."

She chuckled. "Asshole."

The lights dimmed when the decrepit air conditioner kicked back on with a sputter and a low-level hum. "Automatic mood lighting," Levi said as he raised up on all fours. "You pay extra for that?"

She didn't answer but placed her hands on his shoulders and guided him south. He drew his hands down her sides, his thumbs tracing the line down her middle. Down he went, past the patch of precum he'd left above her pubis, through the mat of tight curls at her apex.

Her hips rose up into his touch, wanting, needing so much more. Before critical contact, his lips skipped over her clit. She mewled her frustration, a primal, pitiful sound that made him laugh.

"You are *so* going to pay for tha— *Gah.*"

He dropped his mouth on her, sucking the sensitive nub. Her hands fisted in his hair, pin pricks of pain erupted along his scalp, egging him on. He settled on his stomach, his legs hanging off the end of the bed, but he hardly noticed.

With his tongue, he licked down her slit. She was so hot and wet and ready. He buried his nose in her mound and inhaled her musky scent, vowing to make sure he stuffed his wallet full of condoms and never, ever, left home without them.

She thrust her hips, matching him stroke for stroke, his tongue doing what his dick couldn't. Her moans got shorter, sharper, tiny little puffs of pleasure escaping past the constriction in her vocal cords.

The walls of the motel rooms were thin, and he heard the

television in the next room, the canned laugh track on a sitcom, but he didn't care who overheard them. In fact, he planned on making her scream, on making the guys in the next room turn up the volume to drown them the hell out.

He swapped his tongue for a finger, then added another as she rode him, her wetness making soft sucking sounds that almost had him blowing his load.

Her cries got louder. She was getting close. "That's it, baby," he said as kissed the crease at the top of her inner thigh. "Like that. That's so fucking sexy."

She upped the tempo. He upped his, too. Her hands went to his head, guiding his mouth to her clit. He latched on, the suction sending her over the edge with a shout. He glanced up at her and watched as she tripped into ecstasy.

Levi wiped his face on the sheets and crawled up the length of her body, kissing his way up her neck as she caught her breath. He settled his pelvis against hers, loving the lazy, hazy way she ground up against him.

She ran a hand through her sweat-dampened hair, her words barely a whisper when she said, "Fuck me." The words came out as more of an epitaph than a command.

Levi chuckled, tracing the curve of her ear with his tongue. "I thought I did."

She wrapped her arms around him, pulling him down, taking his full weight.

"I'm not crushing you?"

With firm hands, she stroked up and down the long muscles on either side of his spine. "*Mmmm,*" she said as her hands cupped his ass and tucked him in tighter against her. "I'm not some cracked piece of porcelain you have to handle with care. Besides, I like the way you feel against me."

He didn't have any complaints either. She was tall for a

woman. Slender, yet strong. He liked not having to worry she'd shatter in his hands... unless it was the good kind of shattering.

When she reached a hand down between them, gathered the moisture, and took him in her hand, he didn't complain about that either. He buried his face in the crook of her shoulder, his eyes practically rolling back as she stroked him.

He rose on his forearms, thrusting into the tight space created between her hand and her pelvis, already hot and hard from watching her come, from watching her take pleasure from his hand and his mouth.

Olivia's thumb spread the bead of precum over the rest of the head, his ridge bumping across the edge of her finger again and again.

Her breathing picked up again along with her firm strokes. He rose up a little higher, changing the angle so that his cock also stroked her clit. She gasped, and her body shuddered, her hips finding their own rhythm as she came again. He felt the tingling at the base of him. His thrusts went erratic as he came in her hand and across her abdomen, her belly button filling.

His arms shook as he held his weight off her. Even though she said she liked his weight, a part of him didn't believe he wouldn't crush her. He glanced down, the sight of her covered in his cum almost turned him hard again.

She slid her hand up, catching a drop with her finger that threatened to slip over the edge onto the sheets. With devilment in her eyes, she lifted the finger to her lips and licked it clean.

He groaned, claiming her mouth with his, a touch of his saltiness still on her tongue. "That's hot as hell. You make it awful hard for me not to take you right now. Damn the consequences."

7

Olivia laid on the mattress with Levi stretched out beside her. He rested his head on his hand, one leg tossed casually over hers. Like him, she wanted nothing more than to lose herself in the pleasure, in the sex, in *him*.

Damn the consequences.

Except those consequences could turn into three-year-old little girls.

"Next time," she said.

A furrow formed between his brows as his thoughts turned inward, his fingers ghosting over her chest, down her side, and across her upper abdomen. Still keyed up, her muscles fluttered under his touch.

She played with a lock of his sweat-dampened hair on the nape of his neck, liking the way his sensual gaze grazed her body as if what they'd shared hadn't been a mutual itch that needed scratching, but perhaps something deeper and truer.

Finally, he sucked in a deep breath and scrunched his fingers through the hair at the juncture of her legs. "Do you think there'll be a next time?"

She didn't want to fill him with false hope, since she

was headed back to her ranch first thing Monday morning. But she also wouldn't lie. "I hope so." Then to lighten the mood, she said, "But if it makes you feel any better, you win."

He cracked that sexy, bad-boy cowboy smile and she had to remind of the reasons why a relationship with him could never work. "I win?"

"I told you I wouldn't sleep with you... so..."

"Technically, neither one of us slept."

"True." She laughed, then hazarded a glance at her alarm clock. It was after eleven thirty. "Speaking of sleep... We both have early days tomorrow and we still need to get cleaned up."

Levi grumbled, his hand tracing a delicate circle around her belly. "Do we gotta? I like the way you look—sexy, and sated, and covered in my cum."

She did, too. "Unfortunately."

He rained light kisses onto her forehead, her eyelid, her cheek, the tip of her nose. "Fine," he grumbled. "Ladies first."

"You don't want to join me?"

"More than anything, but I won't be able to keep my hands off you or my dick out of you if I get you wet and lathered."

Levi helped her to her feet before she could forget she was doing the right thing. He sent her to the showers with a swat on her rump. "Save me some hot water."

"We'll see," she said, though only cold water lay in her future. The thought of his large hands on her, soaping her up, made her too hot and bothered as it was.

Quickly, she washed off, enjoying the mild soreness between her legs that had left her wanting more. She came out of the bathroom with a threadbare towel around her body and another turbaned around her head.

Levi was stretched out in her bed completely naked, his head and shoulders propped up on the pillows, a farm and ranch magazine laying across one upturned knee as he skimmed through the pages.

Olivia's gaze went to his crotch. Maybe it was crass, but anyone who saw how endowed he was wouldn't blame her. He cleared his throat and used two fingers to point at his eyes. "Eyes up here. I'm not a piece of meat," he teased.

But the way his cock hardened when she dropped her towel, did make her awfully hungry. He hopped off the other side of the bed before she could get her hands on him. Backing away, he held his hands out in front of him for protection.

He couldn't keep the laughter out of his voice when he said, "I'm trying to be good here. You need to do the same."

"Spoilsport." With big, sad, puppy-dog eyes and a pronounced pout, she plopped belly first onto the bed and retrieved the magazine.

By the time he got out of the shower, she was three pages into an article on the new technologies in the artificial insemination of cattle, which if it worked as well as the article predicted, could be a boon to her bull breeding business. Think of how much more money she could make selling sperm without always having the hassle, dangers, and inconveniences of live covers?

"What are you reading so intently?" He already had his sweatpants on, and he was turning his T-shirt right-side out.

"New technologies in livestock breeding."

"Yeah, fascinating," he said, managing a straight face.

She chucked the magazine at his head, but he was too quick. "It could be really cool," she said, rolling onto her side to face him. "The technology is coming where we could collect semen from bulls and other livestock and ship it cost-effectively around the country or potentially around the world." The possibilities were endless.

He walked over to her, his gaze had gone dark. Leaning over, he planted his hand on her belly where his seed had been and kissed her. Hot and heavy and horny. He broke the kiss before things got out of hand. "You're the only one who can talk about animal breeding and make it sound sexy."

"Get your head out of the gutter."

"I like it there." He sat down on the bed next to her, his hand going to her flank, his thumb tracing tight circles on her hip bone.

"You don't have to leave." His smile faded, and she couldn't read his expression. Had that proclamation come out as pathetic as it sounded? "Never mind. Forget I said anything."

"You don't want me to stay?"

"No. I do. I —" She cut herself off. Refusing to finish that sentence. The one that ended with 'I didn't want you to feel obligated.' Because she wasn't that kind of girl. If she wanted something, she needed to speak up for herself. She looked him in the eye and said. "I want you to stay."

The worry lines on his forehead softened, and he might have had a bit of a smile. He pressed a chaste kiss to her lips. "Me, too."

Levi got up and turned off the overhead light, pitching them into near darkness until her eyes adjusted to the outside light seeping around the edges of the curtains. She heard his clothes hit the floor and she shifted over, making room for him.

He laid out behind her, drawing an arm around her waist and snuggling her up against him.

"This is crazy," she said. "You know that, right? Neither one of us is getting any sleep this way."

He grunted and pulled her in tighter, his arousal settling comfortably against the cleft of her ass. It took everything she had not to wiggle and squirm.

"I should send you home."

His hand moved up, cupping one breast, not as if he were trying to turn her on, but as if he needed the extra contact.

"You should."

But she didn't. And from the way his breathing slowed, he wasn't going anywhere unless she kicked him out of her bed.

She laid there in the dark for an hour, maybe two, too turned on to sleep. Finally, she fell into fitful, erotic dreams that left her waking up in the morning with her hand sliding across his abdomen, headed for what she'd been dreaming about all night.

He sucked in a breath, and his hand clamped down on her wrist. "What do you think you're doing?"

Olivia bumped kisses over his ribs. "I never got to taste you last night." Which technically wasn't true, but...

"What time is it?"

"I set the alarm for six. It hasn't even gone off yet." The second the words were out of her mouth she knew something was wrong. Her room was too light for it to be that early in the morning.

She reached over and snagged her alarm off the bedside table. The clock had stopped a little before three. She whacked it twice and the ticking second hand started again. "Shit," she said. "My alarm messed up."

He rolled out of bed and picked his watch up off the dresser. "It's six forty-five."

Olivia scrambled up and searched through her bag for a pair of panties. "I was supposed to meet Rusty at the barn at six-thirty."

"And I've got fifteen minutes to get to Clive and June's hotel to pick up Clementine."

They were both dressed and out of the motel in minutes. He caught up with her as she pulled open the door of her truck. "Hang on a minute."

"What is it?"

He leaned in, his hair still mussed from sleep, and kissed her. Long and deep until her breathing got ragged and she almost forgot there were places she needed to be. "Have a good day."

————

LEVI STEWED IMPATIENTLY OUTSIDE CLIVE AND JUNE'S MOTEL room. It was seven thirty, and they still hadn't brought Clementine outside. It didn't take thirty minutes to toss clothes on a three-year-old and gather the tiny bag of belongings Olivia had sent with her.

Finally, *finally*, the door to room one-oh-six opened, and Clive, June, and Clementine walked out.

"Lebi!" Clementine called out.

When she attempted to go to him, June caught her hand. "Wait a minute, Clementine. We talked about this."

Clive looked a little pale and refused to acknowledge Levi.

Levi stiffened. "You talked about what?"

"*We*," June said, though, by the pinched expression on Clive's face, June really meant *she*, "think it would be best if Clementine stayed with us."

"I don't understand. I thought you two needed to get back home this morning. Has something changed?"

Clive still wouldn't meet Levi's gaze.

"Clive? What's going on?"

"I didn't mean we think she should stay with us for the day," June said, "We think she should stay with us... permanently."

Permanently?

June might as well have swung a bat and hit him in the head because the word made his head sting and his knees want to buckle. He held onto the bull bars on the front of his truck. "That's not going to happen."

"Be reasonable, son." Clive must have found his tongue. Or his backbone.

Levi ignored him. To Clementine, he said as calmly as he could, "Come on, Pix, we've got to go feed Chunk."

June kept her hand on Clementine's shoulder, restraining her.

"Let her go." He didn't yell or shout or even raise his voice, but his tone conveyed the you-don't-want-to-fuck-with-me message.

"*June*," Clive said, "Do what the man says."

June released Clementine. Only about ten feet separated them, but Levi met her half-way, not taking any chances Clive or June would change their minds.

"This isn't right," June said, "she belongs with us."

Levi picked up his daughter and held on tight. "She stays with me. I'm her father. *I* have sole custody."

June *harrumphed*, that lemon-sucking, pissy-pucker screwing up her face. "We'll see about that."

———

"Really. We don't mind taking her." Ian leaned out of his camper and took Clementine's pink backpack out of Levi's hand as Clementine scurried up the steps.

It was Sunday night and between the rodeo and his responsibilities to Clementine, and Olivia with her responsibilities with her stock and her men preparing for her leaving, they'd hardly had a chance to talk since they'd crawled out of bed together the morning before.

He planned on changing that tonight.

"I wouldn't ask, except this is Olivia's last night." Levi didn't elaborate. No explanation needed. "I won't stay too late."

Cora popped her head out. "Late is fine."

"It's not like that." Expect that it was. It was *exactly* like that.

Ian busted out laughing. "Sure, man."

Levi tagged Ian's shoulder with his fist, not hard enough to really hurt. "Don't be a di—dork. "

Levi squatted down. "Give me a hug, Pix."

She skip-a-loped over to the camper door. A three-year-old's version of a loping horse, because if Chunk did it, she needed to do it too. At least Levi had managed to nip her hay munching proclivities in the bud. Her arms wrapped around his neck and he kissed her cheek.

"Be good for Ian and Cora, okay?"

"*Lebi*." She laid a hand on her hip, having perfected the don't-be-a-dummy tone. Yup, he definitely needed to find babysitters out of their teens.

He pulled a piece of paper out of his pocket and handed it to Ian. "Here's the phone and room number of Olivia's motel in case you need anything."

Ian handed the paper over to Cora for safekeeping. She shooed Levi away. "Now, go. We've got this covered. "

"Okay." Levi took a step back. "Thanks again."

Cora had already disappeared into the camper to help Clementine with something, but Ian said, "Sure thing."

He'd almost made it back to his truck when Cora called out to him. "Hey, Levi."

Turning, he watched as she ran down out of the camper. Ian went inside and closed the door behind her. "Yeah?"

She caught up with him. "I wanted to say that I'm happy for you. I'm glad that you've found what Ian and I have."

"Don't be getting ahead of yourself now."

"Come on." She took a step closer and used her you-can-tell-me-the-truth voice. "It's me you're talking to."

He ducked his head not wanting her to see how much he wanted her words to be true. He couldn't admit what was in his heart, because it seemed too new, too fragile, too fleeting to say out loud and tempt fate, he said, "Ian's good for you."

"Yes, he is." Cora had that little smile on her face saying she would let him get away with his not-so-subtle change of subject. "It's better this way, yeah?"

"Yeah." It had taken him meeting Olivia to see that as terrific as Cora was, she wasn't the right person for *him*.

Unlike Olivia?

Honestly, he couldn't say. Not for sure. It was way too early for that. But he'd sure as hell like the chance to find out.

She gave him a hug and a peck on the cheek. "Don't come back until morning."

He chuckled as he opened the driver's side door. "Yes, ma'am."

When Levi pulled up in front of Olivia's motel room, her truck was nowhere to be found. He glanced at the single red rose and the large box of condoms with the bow on it. Did Olivia even like flowers? Was the box of condoms presumptuous?

She did say next *time.*

Palming both items, he climbed out of the truck and knocked on her door. He hadn't seen her truck in the rodeo parking lot either, but he hadn't really been looking and could have easily missed it. Had Rusty or one of the other guys dropped her off at the motel?

A woman who must have been in her late forties opened the door in nothing but a loosely-belted robe and teased-up hair that she'd lacquered so heavily with hairspray she'd probably burst into flames if the tip of her cigarette got too close.

She took a long, lung-filling drag, her gaze going to the items in his hand. Eyes squinting, she blew the smoke off to one side. "I like a man who comes prepared. You my ten o'clock?"

"No."

"Shame." She sounded more like Clint Eastwood than

Lauren Bacall. "A young stud like you? Hell, handsome, I'd almost pay you."

"I'm just looking for a friend. Olivia Marsh."

"Never heard of her."

"Thank you, anyway." Levi tipped his hat.

"I'm here until morning, love. If you change your mind."

"Good to know," he said as he headed to see the desk clerk. His stomach had a queasy, uneasy feeling. Where had Olivia gone?

He stepped into the motel lobby and banged his palm down on the little bell at the counter. An old man toddled out of the backroom.

"Trish is in room one-oh-six," he said when he saw the box of condoms Levi still had in his hand. The guy may have been old, but his eyes were still sharp.

"I'm looking for the woman who had the room before her. Olivia Marsh."

"Ain't here."

"I'm starting to get that. Did she check out this morning?"

The old man coughed up a ball of phlegm and swallowed it down. "Nah. She was paid through the morning but left late this afternoon."

"What time?"

"Hell, boy. I don't remember. Early enough that Trish still hadn't found a motel for the night. She's a good one, that woman. She don't care if the room ain't exactly clean as long as it's cheap. She does me favors sometimes, if you know what I mean." The old man winked. "I like to return the favor when I can."

"You know prostitution is illegal, right?" Not that Levi really cared, but it wasn't like the old man or Trish were exactly trying to keep what was going in that room quiet.

"Aw hell, boy. A girl's gotta make herself a livin', right? She ain't doing nothing but putting a smile on a man's face. Nothing wrong with that."

Considering he was looking for a particular woman to put a smile on his face, and for him to put one on hers, he couldn't exactly argue the point. "Thanks for the help."

"I hope you find her, son."

"Me too."

————

IN THE PRE-DAWN HOURS OF MONDAY MORNING, OLIVIA stripped her dirty coveralls to her waist and rinsed blood and amniotic fluid off her arms with soap and a bucket of hot water. She glanced over at the mare and foal. The new mother nudged her baby as it tried to stand for the first time.

This was why she needed to be home. This wasn't the kind of physical work her grandfather could do anymore but try telling *him* that.

Earlier that day, she'd received a call at the rodeo office telling her that her grandfather had fallen off the tractor and broken his arm. It hadn't been good news but being there to bring him home from the doctor and being home to help her favorite mare with a difficult, possibly deadly delivery, had been fortuitous.

The fact that she'd been able to completely avoid an awkward goodbye with Levi where she could have screwed it up and not said enough, or worse, said too much, was a plus as well. Levi had enough distractions in his life, he wouldn't want a needy girlfriend added to the mix.

Girlfriend? Aren't you getting a little ahead of yourself there? You kissed and...

She'd done a hell of a lot more than kiss. And a lot less than what she wanted to do. So maybe girlfriend was a stretch, but *friend* was no longer a sufficient label either.

The foal tried to stand on shaky, wobbly legs and crashed to his knees. Olivia watched and waited until the foal stood and stumbled over to his mamma's udder and started suckling.

She heard the scuff of her grandfather's boot on the barn porch and glanced up. He had his newly casted arm in a sling, his leathery cheeks looked more hollow than usual, and the pain meds had stripped the shine from his eyes.

"What are you doing out here? You're supposed to be taking it easy."

Her grandfather was pushing eighty, but if she even tried to hint that maybe, possibly, rightly, he should slow down a bit and let others take up a bit of the slack, he got offended. Then he got downright mad.

But apparently, the painkillers had taken a bit of the edge off his temper because he didn't get mad, he just said, "Stop trying to mother me. I didn't take too kindly to it the first go around. Not likely I'm gonna take to it a second time."

"You broke your arm, for Pete's sake. It's okay to sit still for five minutes. The world's not going to stop turning, old man."

He chuckled. "You get to be my age, and one day soon it's gonna."

Olivia barked out a laugh. "You're too ornery to die."

"That's the plan." Then he hitched a thumb toward the house. "Phone call for ya."

"This early in the morning?" She stripped out of the coveralls the rest of the way, wiping at a smudge of blood that had soaked through to her T-shirt. "Is Rusty having problems with Toot Sweet again? I swear that bull—"

"Ain't Rusty. It's that man of yours, Levi."

Over the past few weeks when she'd called to check on her grandfather, she'd given him the condensed version of Levi and

Clementine's situation, though she hadn't said anything about she and Levi getting together.

"He's not mine."

Her grandfather merely grunted.

They started walking back to the house, then she picked up speed because she didn't know how much money Levi would have to feed into the pay phone for the long-distance call.

"Something wrong with Clementine?"

"He don't sound like a man wanting to talk about his kid. Look, I know you're a grown woman. And I know you don't need an old man digging around in your personal business—"

"When have you ever let that stop you?"

"All I'm saying is this is messy, and with Clive and June as Clementine's grandparents, it's only going to get messier. You don't need anyone dragging you through that. There's a reason your mother cut off contact with June."

"What do you expect me to do? Clementine's kin."

"From the sound of that man's voice, the call has nothing to do with Clementine. Whatever you two got going on, you need to end it now before you break his heart, or he breaks yours."

"It's not like that," she said for the fifth or sixth or twentieth time that night. Mostly to herself.

Despite his age, the painkillers, and the broken arm, her grandfather beat her up the steps to the old house and held open the door for her. "Two days after I said that same thing to my old man, I got down on one knee and proposed to your grandmother."

"You don't have to worry. There are no proposals in my near future." Or in the far future either. Not when she had the ranch to run.

She boosted herself onto the kitchen counter and picked up the receiver her grandfather had laid to the side. If her grandmother had been alive to see her jump on the counter, she would have given Olivia a swat to the butt with a rolled-up dish-towel. Her grandfather had always let Olivia get away with it, even though over the years she'd left scuff marks and dings on the side of the cabinets from her spurs and her boot heels.

"Hello?" she said.

The line popped and cracked, but she heard the force of Levi's exhaled breath. "You left." Not a question. An accusation.

"My grandfather broke his arm. I had to get back. Someone had to take care of the animals and the rest of the ranch. He's old and—"

"I ain't so old I can't hear you, missy," her grandfather called out from the couch, as he attempted to read the newspaper with one hand.

Olivia didn't respond to her grandfather, not that he would have expected her to. To Levi, she said, "I'm needed here. I came home."

"Five minutes." Levi's accusatory tone had shifted to something softer. "The ranch could have survived you taking five extra minutes to come find Clementine to say goodbye to her. To me."

"You're mad."

"Wouldn't you be? If the situation was reversed? If after spending that night together, I'd vanished?"

"My leaving had nothing to do with that... that morning." *You sure about that? Can you say that and look at yourself in the mirror at the same time?* "I was already coming home. I just left a day early."

The pops and buzzing on the line filled the silence. She bumped her head against the upper cabinet, over and over again, hoping to knock sense into herself, because what she wanted to do was climb back into her truck and make the long drive back to East Texas.

"No," Levi said at last. The single word came out so low, she had to strain to hear him over the line. "You ran."

More pops. Hisses. The operator came on and demanded more money.

After the final coin dropped, he said, "What are you afraid of, Liv?"

8

WHAT ARE YOU AFRAID OF, LIV?

Levi never got an answer to his question. Instead, she'd muttered about it being late and her being beat and could they maybe talk about it another time.

Levi took it as the brush off that it was, blaming his little infatuation with Olivia as his brain's tricky way of trying to come to terms with the emotions that had been rattling around in his head since Clementine had come roaring into his life.

No way had he developed genuine feelings for the woman in such a short time. It was the stress and the circumstances that had brought them together.

Levi led Chunk to his two-horse bumper pull trailer now attached to his truck. Clementine walked beside him. It was almost noon, and most of the competitors had already left for the next weekend's rodeo in Oklahoma City. But it was an easy drive, one he could make in a day, even with a three-year-old in tow, so after he'd picked up Clementine early from a curious Ian and Cora, he'd decided they'd sleep in. As late as a man with a rambunctious little girl could.

If nothing else, Clementine had enjoyed the pony ride

Chunk had given her as Levi led him around and around one of the outside arenas. For once, they hadn't been in a mad rush to pack up and get on the road. Which wasn't like him. Usually, he was one of the first guys out after the rodeo ended and one of the first guys at the next location, ready to practice. Ready to win.

Funny how your priorities shifted when you had little sticky fingers around your neck and those precocious blue eyes staring up at you each day.

Levi pinned open the rear doors of the trailer. "Stay right here," he told Clementine as he stood her out of the way beside the far door. "Don't move until I tell you to, okay?"

She nodded. But she was three, so he kept his eye on her as he tossed Chunk's lead rope over his back and sent him into the trailer. He pinned the butt bar into place to keep Chunk from backing out and closed the half door behind his horse.

Then he turned to Clementine who'd for once, stayed where he'd put her. "Pix, you undo the latch, and we'll close the other door."

She scurried around the door, tugging on the latch, but it wouldn't budge. He pointed to the latch release. "Push there, then pull up on the latch."

Her tongue went to the corner of her mouth as she pushed on the spring-activated lever as hard as she could. He was about to give her a hand when it released, and the latch popped free.

"Me did it."

"Good job, baby." He held out his hand, and she gave it a slap before she used all her strength to push the door closed.

Levi secured the latch and gave both doors a little tug to make sure they were secure.

Someone cleared his throat behind Levi. "Are you Levi Banks?"

Levi turned to find a guy in a suit. Levi picked up Clementine and rested her on his hip. She gave the man her widest smile and her rodeo queen wave.

In Levi's experience, suited strangers never approached with good news. He thought about saying, 'who's asking?' but that would pretty much give him away. "I'm Banks."

The man handed him a manila envelope. "You've been served."

"What the hell is this?" Levi asked as he worked the sealed flap of the envelope.

"That's a bad word, Lebi."

"Sorry, Pix."

He leveled his gaze at the stranger.

The guy said, "I deliver them. I don't know what's inside. Have a good day."

Levi could only muster a grunt as he pulled the papers out. He put Clementine down and sat on the wheel well of his trailer while Clementine went around and around under the bridge his legs made.

He had to read the papers three times for the words to finally sink in and the anger to go from a slow simmer to a bubbling boil. He shoved the papers back into the envelope, got his spare change from the ashtray of the truck, and jogged with Clementine back to the pay phones by the rodeo office.

With shaking hands, it took him several tries to get the money in the slot. He kept his eye on Clementine as she climbed the first rung on the empty pen across from him. "Don't go any higher."

She tilted her head back, her weight on her outstretched arms as she looked at him upside down.

He'd better make the call quick or else she'd get bored and scramble to the top of the pen in no time. Whoever had said little girls were easier to handle than boys never had one.

The phone buzzed and buzzed and buzzed until finally, someone answered.

"Hello?" It was Olivia.

"It's me," he said without preamble. "I need help. June and Clive are suing me for custody."

"They're *what?*"

"They're suing for custody. I got served papers in the parking lot of the rodeo grounds. How the hell did that happen so fast? They were just here on Saturday."

"Clive is good friends with one of the deacons at their church. He's a pretty powerful, well-connected lawyer in these parts. Lawyers can move fast when they want to."

Levi caught movement out of the corner of his eye and glanced up. "Stop right there, young lady." Clementine had almost climbed her way to the top. "Hang on a minute," he said to Olivia. "I gotta get Clementine before she falls and cracks her skull open. Wouldn't that be great ammunition to present to the judge?"

When he returned to the phone with his daughter on his shoulders, Olivia said, "Come to the ranch. Clive isn't the only one who has lawyers for friends."

"Olivia, I don't have that kind of money. I've got a little bit put away, but—"

"Come to the ranch," she repeated. She had that no-nonsense, take-charge tone that he'd always found so damn sexy. "We'll talk to our own lawyer and we'll figure out what we need to do from there."

There she was again, using 'we' and 'our' like they were in this mess together. He had to remember one thing... she'd been the one who'd run.

"I guess I've got a few days I can spare. I could leave early Friday morning for Oklahoma City and still make the go for that night, if it takes a few days to get things sorted."

He had to shove in more quarters to keep the connection open long enough for Olivia to give him directions to the ranch. He scribbled the address on the back of someone's flier pinned to the bulletin board. He found concentrating difficult while Clementine used the top of his head as a bongo drum. He read the instructions back to Olivia.

"That's it," she said, "The dirt road we're off can be hard to find. If you hit the Llano river, turn around, you've gone too far."

"Okay. I think I've got it."

"I guess I'll see you in a few hours."

"Yeah. And Liv? Clementine really missed you this morning." Clearly, something about the direction their relationship had turned had freaked her out. He wasn't going to make the situation worse by telling Olivia he'd missed her, too.

"Same here."

Before she could hang up, he added, "One more thing."

There was a hesitation on her end, and her voice softened when she said, "What's that?"

"I appreciate the help. Before. And now. I'm starting to wonder what I'd do without you."

———

"They're here," Olivia's grandfather said, as he walked out onto the front porch, the rickety screen door slapping against the jamb behind him. One of these days, Olivia would get around to tightening the hinge screws and putting in the new screen that had been sitting in the barn unopened for the past six months.

Olivia finished washing the dirt and grease off her fingers from changing the oil in the old tractor and dried her hands on her jeans as she walked to the front door. She glanced in the mirror and snatched the errant piece of hay out of her messy ponytail. A smudge of grease sat above her right eye that spit and a rub with her thumb couldn't erase. But the hell with it. She had no one she was trying to impress.

Not that she *would* impress anybody in her old work boots, a tattered pair of jeans, and one of her grandfather's old western shirts tied at the waist over a T-shirt to protect it from oil stains.

She leaned on the porch rail and waited as Levi followed the drive past the house and brought his rig to a stop near the barn. Olivia trotted down the steps after him. Her grandfather on her heels.

Levi climbed out, and her grandfather went for the passenger door. "Let me get Clementine out," Olivia said. "I don't want you to hurt your arm."

Her grandfather cut her a look. "I think I can handle a door latch without re-injuring myself."

"Fine." She held her hands up in surrender and turned her attention to Levi. "How was the drive?"

He plunked his hat on his head and stretched his back. "We're getting the hang of this road trip thing. Only had to stop three times to pee. Two were false alarms."

"Grampy Joe." Clementine's grin stretched across her face, showing off two rows of bright white baby teeth. Olivia's grandfather held her hand as she jumped out of the truck.

Levi came around the hood and held his hand out to Olivia's grandfather. "Levi Banks. I appreciate you putting us up for a few days, Mr. Marsh."

"Call me Joe," her grandfather said. "And we're happy to help."

Clementine stood with one foot on her grampy's boot, leaning back as far as she could with one hand in his, swinging back and forth.

"I didn't realize you and Clementine had met."

"Despite the rift in the family, Mae and Clementine were

always welcome, and Olivia did her fair share of babysitting over the years to help first Mae, and then Randy, out."

"I appreciate you watching out for my girls."

Mae and Clementine?

Then he caught Olivia's eye over her grandfather's shoulder.

Had he included her?

Did he consider her one of *his* girls?

Or was that wishful thinking?

As good as her grandfather's ears were, his eyes were just as good, catching the brief look they'd shared. "Dinner's ready in fifteen. You kids put the horse up. I'll get Clem cleaned up for dinner."

The way Levi eyed her, she wasn't certain she wanted to be alone with him. A spark of that anger she'd heard in his voice last night when he'd confronted her about the way she'd left was still in his eyes. But what spooked her the most was the hurt deeper in those depths.

She didn't want to admit she had the power to hurt him, because if she had that kind of power, that meant they had a relationship. And if they had a relationship... then he had the power to hurt her, too.

"I can take Clementine," she offered.

"I've got her," her grandfather insisted as he took Clementine's hand and started for the house.

Levi passed by her on his way to the rear of the trailer. "Nice try, boss."

"I'm not your boss," she grumbled. But not too loud because she kind of liked the rough, gruff way it rolled off his tongue.

She opened the second door and stepped into the empty stall and untied Chunk's lead rope while Levi opened the other door and unhooked the butt bar.

"You can throw the end of the rope over his back," Levi said.

When she did, Levi clucked, and Chunk cautiously backed

out. After his front feet hit the ground, Chunk sniffed the air and whinnied. One of the horses in the barn answered back as Levi gathered up the lead rope and headed toward the barn.

Olivia pointed to a paddock behind the barn. "We can put him in there. He can have it to himself and meet the other horses over the fence line. There's plenty of grass and room for him to run and stretch his legs."

"Sounds good."

They walked side by side, but the tension between them made the muscles between her shoulder blades knot and the saliva dry up in her mouth.

He didn't say anything while he released Chunk into the paddock, or while they checked water troughs, or while they placed a few flakes of hay in the feeder.

She couldn't take it any longer. She closed the paddock gate and caught his arm. "Look, Levi, about yesterday…"

He turned, his expression both a little sad and thoughtful. "Tell you what. I'm tired, and hungry, and doing my best to keep my shit together considering that envelope of papers sitting on the dashboard of my truck. As much as I want to have this conversation *and* the explanation, can we wait until after Clementine has gone to bed? Until then, truce?"

She could do that. She owed him that much. "Truce."

His expression softened, and that twitch at the corners of his lips might have been a fractional smile. Levi backed her up against the fence post, his fingers linking behind her neck, his thumbs brushing across her pulse points. He bent his head to hers, their lips almost touching. "I'm going to kiss you, Olivia Marsh."

He waited a fraction of a second, time enough for her to tell him no. But she didn't want to refuse him. She rose on her toes and closed the gap. He made a sound, part surprise, part desire, all sexy.

Her hands went to his chest, to the thump of his heart against her palms. As she angled her head, opening her mouth to his, emotion poured in, in the angry way his tongue danced with hers, in the hurt in the light nip to her bottom lip, in the uncertain way his fingers traced down the sides of her face, in the trepidation when he pulled back and tentatively went back for more.

When their breathing got heavy, he broke the kiss, touching his forehead to hers. "I missed those lips." His voice went gruff and he swallowed hard as if he had something difficult to say, but the words never came.

He pressed a kiss to the side of her head. "Come on. We don't want to keep dinner waiting."

They walked back to the house, two fingers loosely linked. By the time they got inside, her grandfather had the table set and had placed the salad and potatoes in the center of the table.

"I need a hand getting the pot roast out of the oven," her grandfather said. "Then we'll be ready to eat."

"I'll get it." Levi washed up at the sink. "The three of you sit down."

There wasn't much room in the eat-in breakfast area. Olivia put Clementine in a booster seat she had bought for those times when Clementine had stayed at the ranch. Her grandfather sat across from her at the four-seater square table. Olivia served the potatoes and salad and took her own seat. Levi plopped the pot roast he'd sliced onto the table.

Clementine grabbed a slice of meat from the platter he'd set too close to her and slid it onto her plate.

"Let your daddy cut that, Clem," Olivia's grandfather said.

Levi stilled, his fork dropping to his plate.

Olivia said, "Uh, oh."

"Mommy and daddy are in heaben. I have Lebi."

Levi turned a light shade of green. "Mae told her I was dead?"

"Clementine doesn't know you're her father?" Her grandfather whispered, but Clementine's ears were even better than his.

"*Grampy*," Olivia said, through gritted teeth.

Clementine glanced at Levi, then around the rest of the table, knowing something was up but way too young to fully understand.

To her grandfather, Levi said, "I figured she had enough to adjust to in the beginning without throwing that tidbit into the mix, so if you could just—"

"Lebi my daddy?"

Levi closed his eyes a pained moment. When he opened them, he looked straight at Olivia, and she was sure that the word on the tip of his tongue was an emphatic *fuuuck*. Slowly, carefully, Levi wiped his hands on his napkin even though he'd yet had a chance to touch his food.

"Yes, Pix. I'm your daddy. Is that okay with you?" The forced levity wasn't lost on his daughter. Clementine cocked her head as he gave her a reassuring smile. Levi picked up his knife and fork and started slicing her meat into finger-sized bites.

Olivia had expected Clementine to clap or smile or even let loose with an excited 'yippee'—a word Clementine had started using the week before—but Clementine picked up a piece of meat and put it in her mouth, the wheels still churning in her head.

"Yes? No?" Levi prompted his daughter.

Clementine nodded. She didn't look sad, or happy. Just... thoughtful.

Levi glanced over at Olivia. She shrugged, not knowing what to make of his daughter's reaction either.

"My apologies," her grandfather said.

Levi nodded his acceptance, but for the rest of the dinner,

conversation remained stilted, and despite how hungry Levi had claimed to be, he barely touched his food. Clementine dozed on and off in her seat, taking the occasional bite after she'd eaten most of what she'd been served.

When Olivia and her grandfather finished eating, she started clearing the plates and told Levi, "I made up a cot in the guest room for her, and she has her own towels in the bathroom at the end of the hall if you want to get her ready for bed. And I think there might be a pair of her pajamas still in the dresser in there."

Levi pushed away from the table and went to take Clementine in his arms. "Yeah. Poor thing. These trips really wear her out."

After she'd finished washing the dishes and cleaning the kitchen, she searched for Levi and Clementine. She'd half expected the bath to give Clementine a second wind, and that Clementine would be raring to go late into the night, but Olivia hadn't heard much noise from the end of the hall.

From the hallway, she heard the soft murmur of Levi's voice. She stopped in the doorway of the guest room and saw Levi sitting on the floor in the darkness, an arm over an upraised knee, his other hand on his daughter's head with his thumb brushing softly across her forehead.

"So, you're okay with me being your daddy?"

Clementine nodded. It wasn't like Clementine to be so quiet, even when she was tired. The news must have been a lot for her to take in, even at three.

"Lebi?"

"Yeah, Pix."

"When is mommy coming back from heaben?"

Levi stilled, then blew out a long breath. "As much as she loved you and would like to be here, Mommy's not coming back, Pix. That's not how it works."

"You came back."

Olivia's heart cracked, and the tightness in her chest made breathing next to impossible. She must have made a noise, because Levi glanced over, the pain in his expression a looming, palpable entity. The slight shake of his head said, 'I don't know what to say to that.'

Then he turned back to his daughter and after a few moments said, "I was gone, but I wasn't in heaven. But I'm here now, and I pinkie promise I'm not going away again. Okay?"

"'Kay."

He leaned in and kissed her on the forehead. "Night, night, Pix. I love you."

"Lub you, too, Lebi."

After hearing those words, he rubbed at his sternum as if trying to ease a pain in his chest, though he seemed unaware he was doing it. Slowly he stood, somehow looking exhausted, gutted, and elated at the same time. Right then and there, Olivia vowed to do whatever she could to make sure June and Clive never took Clementine from her father. Levi and Clementine deserved better than that.

Levi met Olivia at the door. His expression was enigmatic. Putting her arm around his waist, she whispered, "You okay?"

He chuckled, more sad than sincere as he wrapped his arm around her shoulders and walked her back down the hall. "I don't know yet. Joe got anything to drink around here?"

9

———

"Where's Joe?" Levi asked as he set the bottle of whiskey and two glasses on the coffee table in front of the couch.

The kitchen lights spilling into the unlit den. The two-seater, worn leather couch, the coffee table, and a recliner filled the room. In the corner sat a small television with tinfoil on the rabbit ears. He sat down and poured them both two fingers of Joe's Black Label whiskey,

"I sent him to the VFW hall." Olivia pulled off her boots and sat in the corner of the couch next to him, her legs tucked beneath her. "The widow Warren plays bingo on Monday nights. He's sweet on her."

"Does that mean we shouldn't wait up?"

"Probably not."

Levi chuckled and handed Olivia her glass. "Here's to the old dog and new tricks."

Olivia laughed, clinking her glass against his before taking a sip. "May we never be too old for love."

They lapsed into silence and let the whiskey do its thing. Olivia sank lower into the cushions, facing him and resting the side of her head against the back of the couch. "Sorry about

Gramps. He didn't know, and I didn't think to tell him otherwise."

"It's okay. It's probably better this way. I wanted Clementine to know I'm her father, but I wasn't sure how to bring it up. She's smart but she is only three. How much of it can she really understand?"

"The important thing for her to know is that she's wanted and that she's loved. You show that to her every day. *That* even a three-year-old can understand."

"You're right." He swirled the whiskey with the ice cubes in his glass before taking a sip. It took everything he had in him, including the whiskey, for him to say, "I'm terrified June and Clive are going to win. I can't lose Clementine. I promised I'd be there for her. I don't plan on breaking my word."

Olivia set her glass on the coffee table. She took his hand and made sure she had his full attention. "You're not going to lose her. We have an appointment with a damn fine lawyer first thing in the morning. We're going to fight this and we're going to win."

There was that 'we' again. As much as he liked the sound of that, he couldn't let go of the way she'd left the day before. No goodbye. No nothing. That didn't sound like a 'we' to him.

So, he called her on it. "We. You say that like we're together. That we're a package deal..." He slurped down the rest of his whiskey and poured himself another. "I went to your motel room last night. When you weren't there... When the desk clerk said you'd checked out early..." he shook his head. Damn. It shouldn't be that difficult to say out loud. "I didn't know what to think."

He took another gulp, and a portion of the anger and frustration he'd kept bottled up leaked out. The more he thought about it, the more he realized he couldn't leave the conversation there. It didn't do a damn bit of good to talk about it if he didn't say what was on his mind. "No scratch that. I *do* know what I thought. I thought whatever it was we'd started was over. Finished. And now here you are... using words like 'we' and I guess it's *now* that I don't know what to think."

"I think it's time I gave you that apology." Olivia's voice had grown soft and her expression sheepish. "I could have handled leaving a lot better."

Levi raised a brow at her. "Ya think?"

She chuckled when she said, "You're such an ass."

Then she took a sip of his drink and set it on the coffee table next to hers. She straddled him on the couch and wrapped her arms around his neck. "You asked me on the phone what I'm afraid of, and honestly, I don't know. You. Me. Clementine. My life here. Yours on the road. It's got 'never-gonna-work' written all over it, but then there are times when it's just you and me and Clementine... that's when I ask myself 'why not?'"

He shouldn't, wouldn't, couldn't get his hopes up. It felt like he was standing in the middle of an arena with nothing but a red cape and an angry bull. One false move could turn into a disaster.

"We don't have to get ahead of ourselves, plan out five, ten, or fifteen years into the future. We need to get through today and then tomorrow and then the next day and the day after that. One day at a time. We'll make it work until it doesn't."

He held her hips and pulled her tighter against him as her fingers traced tiny circles on the nape of his neck.

"I guess it's the 'until it doesn't' that I'm afraid of. You've foul-hooked my heart, Banks, and I'm afraid you're going to rip it right out of my chest."

"The feeling's mutual." This wasn't a time to play it coy or hold his cards close to his chest. It didn't seem like they had that kind of luxury, not with the odds stacked against him like the back, back room of an off-the-strip Vegas casino. "We'd better make this thing work then or else we're looking at our mutual destruction."

She laughed. "Did you just equate our relationship to a nuclear standoff?"

"Only this has the potential to end much worse."

Olivia trailed a hand down his chest, and it landed on his belt buckle. "Or potentially much better."

He grabbed her hand. "Hold that thought."

She gave a small whine of displeasure.

"Why don't we go somewhere a little more private, in case Joe decides to come home early. Go to your room, I'll meet you there."

She leaned back far enough to see his face. "Where are you going?"

"To the truck. I brought you a little something."

———

WHILE LEVI WENT TO HIS TRUCK, OLIVIA NIPPED INTO THE shower. He'd have to be messed up to think the scents of motor oil and horse sweat were a kinky aphrodisiac.

She left her dirty clothes in the hamper in the bathroom and tiptoed in her towel past Clementine's partially open door into her bedroom. Even though Gramps wasn't home, she was glad her room was across the hall and down one from his because the house was old, and his ears were still too good.

Levi was already in her room when she got there, his torso and feet bare. His back was to her, as he studied frame after frame of pictures and awards from her childhood. She didn't bother turning on the overhead light, the soft glow from the bedside table lamp provided more than enough visibility for what they had in mind.

"Hey there." She closed and locked the door. They didn't

need Clementine, or God forbid, her grandfather to walk in on them.

He turned, with a box in his hands, the ribbon a little smashed and lopsided. "For you."

She held the box of condoms up to the light and laughed. "I would say you shouldn't have but I'm damn glad you did."

"You are?"

"Sure," she teased, "when the local guys hear that I'm back in town—"

Levi made a sound, a possessive growl of disapproval that should have annoyed her, but the sound made her hot. A muscular arm shot out and wrapped around her waist, holding her tight against him. Into her ear, he whispered, "I don't share. My condoms or my woman."

"I thought they were *my* condoms. Are you taking back your gift?"

"I'll tell you what," he said, his eyes smiling, his grin as wide as Llano County. "I'll make you a deal. If, after we polish off this box, you still want to bang other men, I'll buy you another box myself."

"Cocky much?" She laughed, but the joke was on her. She had no desire to screw other men, but *he* didn't have to know that.

He answered with a kiss so deep, so long, so consuming it had her arms coming around his neck, drawing soft moans of pleasure and leaving her wanting to climb him like a tree. When he finally pulled away, he said, "Confident, not cocky."

He took the box from her hand. "You mind?"

She shifted until she straddled one of his thighs, her fingers trailing across the waistband of his Wranglers. "Not if you hurry."

Deftly, he ripped through the ribbon and used his teeth to tear the outer cellophane wrapper.

"That's a pretty big box," she said. Not that she was complaining.

"I've been accused a time or two of being too ambitious. I won't apologize for that."

She grinned. "Ambition is admirable."

Finally, he pulled a condom free and set it and the rest of the box on the desk beside him. The same old oak desk that she'd had since grade school. She had to admit, she liked it better covered in condoms than construction paper.

Resting a hip against the corner of the desk, he leaned in and kissed and nipped his way down her neck. She let her head fall back, giving him full access, but when his hands went to the tucked corner of her towel, she stopped him. "You first."

His tongue trailed the length of her collarbone. "Me first, huh? Why's that?"

"I want to see you." She palmed the condom and sat down on the corner of her bed.

He reached for his belt buckle. "Fair enough."

Though he was the one stripping, the way he watched her, the way his gaze glided down her torso, touching, almost caressing her with his intensity, made her feel like the naked one. She could feel the places he wanted to squeeze and suck and fuck.

He teased her, making a play of undressing by taking his jeans off first then going back for his underwear, the bulge of his half-hard shaft made it impossible not to stare.

Not that she was really trying.

Then he pulled the thin cotton fabric to his ankles and kicked it aside. He stood there in front of her, his hands at his sides, his erection growing by the second. She wanted to reach for the overhead light switch, to see him in his naked, luscious, colossal, glory but didn't want to break the mood. She ripped the corner off the square package in her hand and took out the condom.

She shifted on the bed, his eyes going dark and his smile going feral when she spread her legs and ground against the corner of the mattress. Feeling emboldened, she said, "Stroke yourself."

His eyes smoldered, and he took a step toward her.

"Ah, ah." She held out a staying hand. "That's as close as you get."

He raised one dark brow, and one side of his wicked mouth curved up. "Guess I'll have to make you come to me, then."

Instead of reaching for his cock like she'd instructed, he ran a hand across his chest, over the peaks of his pecs and the vast valley in between. "I want your lips here." His fingers eased across to his flat nipples. They hardened as he brushed a thumb over them. "I want your teeth here."

Goosebumps erupted on his skin, and when he had her undivided attention, he let his hand drift ever so slowly downward. "Your tongue here."

Down past the washboard of muscles on his abdomen. "Here."

Down past the circle of hair around his belly button.

Down past the V of muscle angling toward his groin.

Down.

Down until the tips of his fingers dipped into the hair at the apex of his thighs and his cock landed in the web between his thumb and forefinger. "Your hot, wet mouth here."

His voice had dipped so low. It was more grumble than growl. She reached up and pulled the thin cord dangling down from her ceiling fan before she self-combusted. The blades began turning, and the bad bearing in the motor whirred. But the last thing on her mind was yet another item on her fix-it list.

Right now, the only thing that needed her attention was this mountain of a naked man in front of her.

Then his large hand curved around his base, making a slow, long slide to the tip and back again. A drop of precum at his slit begged and begged to be licked away. Before she'd made the conscious decision to go to him, she fell to her knees at his feet. The old wooden floorboards creaked under her weight.

She ghosted her hand over his as it rode up and down his shaft, the dual exploration adding an erotic kick. As if she wasn't already turned on and cranked up to eleven.

With her free hand, she cupped his balls. He hissed in a breath, his other hand going to the back of her head, encouraging her.

He let go of himself when she grabbed the base and gave him a few firm strokes of her own. She glanced up as his head fell back. She breathed in his musky scent, and licked the salty, dewdrop from his tip.

Levi groaned.

As much as she wanted to tease him, Olivia couldn't bring herself to stop there. She laved around the head, her tongue following the ridge around and around.

"Jesus Christ," he moaned, his hips thrusting toward her, wanting, needing more.

Then she opened her mouth and took him down to the base, her throat threatening to spasm as the hard length of him hit the back of her throat. He pulled out a fraction, easing the pressure. She sucked and licked until moisture pooled between her legs. She wanted to knock him to the floor and have her wild, wicked, way with him.

"Oh, baby," Levi said, his voice too gruff to be considered a whisper. "That feels so goddamn good."

She took him deep again. His balls tightened. So close, she wanted to finish him off.

"Come up here," he said. When he went to help her up, she resisted long enough to slip the condom on and roll it down his length. Then she stood, and his mouth came crashing down on hers. Possessing. Owning.

She gave in to the kiss, the passion, letting her emotion fuel the burning need she had for this man.

When their breaths went ragged, and their lungs burned and ached, he broke the kiss. "Turn around."

The look she gave him fell between what's-up-your-sleeve and I'm-not-falling-for-that.

"Trust me," he said as he took her by the shoulders and spun her around to face the desk, "You'll thank me later."

10

***

"Lose the towel," Levi told Olivia as he gave himself a slow pump and then another.

Olivia glanced at him over her shoulder, her damp hair leaving the occasional drip of water down her back. She didn't argue. Her towel dropped to the floor with a soft *whompfh*. He traced a finger down her back, following a drop of water as it slid down the length of her spine until it disappeared into the crack of her ass.

He blew cool air on her skin, sending a rash of goosebumps across her heated flesh. "Bend over." He pressed a gentle hand against her shoulder until her forearms rested on the desk.

Her skin glowed in the soft light, the sight of her cocked over her desk, her ass in the air, almost made him blow his load. It made his heart hurt, and his lungs seize. "You're so stunning."

He ran his hands over her body, from the hard line of her shoulder blades, down the lean muscles along her spine, to the gentle indention at her waist, to the soft curve of her exquisite ass.

He held her hips and pressed himself into that enticing cleft. He could have taken her then as she arched her back, pressing her ass even tighter against him. Holding back, he nudged her feet farther apart. The time would come for that soon enough. Until then, he planned on blowing her mind.

"What are you doing?" She sounded more worked up than worried.

Pressing a kiss between her shoulder blades, he said, "You're about to find out."

He dropped to his knees, using her towel for protection against the bite of the hardwood floors. Olivia let out a long, slow breath, her leg muscles quaking as he ran his hands down the outside of her legs. Then he traced a languorous trail up the inside of her thighs.

Olivia shifted, as if aching for that intimate touch that eased ever so close but never came. She made a sound somewhere between a subtle whine and a disgruntled growl. "Banks, I swear if you don't—"

He dipped his head between her legs, breathing in her scent and tracing her folds with his tongue, loving her taste and how wet she was for him. Her complaints died and were replaced by low moans and breathing that came in hitching huffs and puffs.

Reaching up, he added his broad thumb to the mix as it pushed deep inside, her warmth collapsing around him as his finger traced up her folds and found that taut bundle of nerves.

She bent over further, allowing better access as her hand came around, pressing against the back of his head. He nipped and sucked as she rode his thumb and rubbed up against his finger. The pleasure she took from him made him even harder. He'd planned on making her come that way, but he felt the tingling at the base of his spine, and he knew he'd never last.

He pulled back, giving one ass cheek a playful bite as he stood.

"Don't you dare stop now, Banks." The harshness of her tone was delightfully deadly, and he couldn't wait to be inside her.

He pulled his hand free.

She glared at him over her shoulder.

He smiled. "Tsk, tsk," he said. "Aren't we getting a tad worked up?"

"*You* got me worked up," she groused. "And you damn well better fix it. Now."

God, he loved it when she got aroused, her threats only making him want to drag the torture out longer. But, good and bad, what he did to her was equally torturous for him. He wasn't a masochist. There was only so much self-flagellation that he could take.

He positioned himself at her entrance, prepared for an exquisitely long and slow slide in, but Olivia wasn't a woman who waited to be serviced. She was the type of woman who took what she wanted and didn't apologize for her greediness.

He loved that about her.

In one motion, she thrust back against him until he was balls deep in her warmth, a light flutter of contractions tightened her walls around him. She thumped her forehead against the desk. "You feel—*Oompfh*—"

He pulled out and thrust in again, his hands gripping her hips until he bottomed out inside her.

"Like that," she said.

He wrapped his arms around her waist, holding her to him. Then his hands started roaming up her stomach to the swell of her breasts. He lightly pinched her peaked nipples. Olivia raised her head and she drove her ass deep, deep into his pelvis.

She braced her hands on the edge of the desk for leverage. "Fuck me, Banks."

For support, he braced one hand on her shoulder and the other at her hip, then he did what she so succinctly, so eloquently, so candidly asked for—he fucked her.

His breathing came hot and heavy as he pounded into her,

her counter thrusts taking him incredibly deep. Their powerful strokes made the desk thump into the wall. The pictures in the frames shook, and between the banging on the walls, and Olivia's cries, they were either going to bust through the wall or shatter her grandmother's old crystal in the kitchen. If she had any.

Or worse, wake Clementine.

He slowed, but not before a picture fell onto the desk and tumbled onto the floor. He thought he heard the glass crack. He pulled Olivia up against him, her back to his chest, changing the angle as well as the speed. Her legs quaked, and he reached around to her clit.

"Oh, yeah," she said, her voice sultry, smoky.

"You like that?" He dipped his finger into her wetness and teased the tiny nub.

In place of an answer, she reached a hand back and cupped his head, her other covered his busy hand as she ground against the pressure. Though his thrusts had slowed, they became erratic as he pushed them both toward a climax, the sensations zipping along his spine setting his nerves alight.

Then her body stiffened, and her breath caught, and her walls clamped down around him. He crossed his arms over her chest, holding her tight, thrusting one more time until he, too, took a tumbling swan dive off that high cliff.

Her knees went to rubber, and he took her weight in his arms. He breathed her in again, loving the musky, steamy mix of sweat and sex, and how Olivia gave as good as she got.

He kissed across her shoulder to the crook of her neck. "You're extraordinary."

She chuckled, her breath coming easier. "I could say the same about you, but I'd be afraid it would go straight to your head."

"Best keep it to yourself then."

"Agreed."

He would have liked to have stayed in her for the rest of the night, or the week, or... you know... his life.

This was always a temporary thing. You knew that going in.

Yeah, but knowing it and liking it were two entirely different things.

As he grew soft, he pulled out and disposed of the condom in the trash can under the desk. He picked up the photo that had fallen. She came up beside him, and he wrapped an arm around her shoulder. "First place show steer, not too shabby, Miss FFA Badass."

"Yeah, in this part of Texas, you either play football or join the Future Farmers of America. There's not much middle ground. And since I'm shit at throwing spirals..."

Then he looked again at the pictures. Frame after frame of FFA wins. "You really dominated. There must have been a countywide collective cheer when you aged out of the competition."

She laughed as she ran her fingers across his flank. If she didn't stop that, they'd be on to round two in no time. "I didn't always win first place."

He glanced at a cord stretched across from one side of the room to the other with blue ribbon after blue ribbon clipped to it. "Uh, huh," he said, his bullshit detector set on high. No wonder she had some of the best rodeo stock in the business.

He led her by the hand to her full-sized bed. It was the only thing in the room that didn't look like it had been there since her teenage years.

They adjusted the pillows, and he settled against the headboard, with her back to his chest between his legs. He draped his arms over her shoulders. "Doesn't look like your room's changed much since high school."

"My dad got a new job the summer after my sophomore year. They moved to Chicago but let me stay behind for my junior and senior year. My grandmother helped me redecorate after they moved out. She died not long after. A massive stroke."

"I'm sorry."

"It's okay. It was hard at the time. But Gramps and I got through it together. I haven't been able to bring myself to change anything since she's been gone. I like the reminder of the time we'd spent making this room mine."

"That's sweet."

"Maybe. But kind of a turn off to invite your boyfriend into a kid's room to have sex."

Boyfriend. Levi stiffened.

She tilted her head up to meet his gaze. "Don't freak. I didn't mean it. It's the sex fog talking."

"I wasn't freaking out. I was... surprised." He brought his mouth down on hers for a quick touch, linking his hands with hers. "In fact, I kind of like the sound of it."

"You do?"

The way she said it, he couldn't tell if she was enamored or repulsed by it. He took a chance. "I do."

"Hmmm," she said as she settled back against his chest. "It doesn't sound *too* awful."

He dropped her hands and went after her ribs. She laughed and tried to get away as he tickled her into submission.

"Okay, okay, okay," she said.

He stopped tickling long enough to ask, "Okay, what?"

"I kind of like the sound of it, too."

———

When Olivia woke, it was still dark outside, but it wouldn't be for long. She turned in Levi's arms, loving the tenderness between her thighs and the way their bodies fit together. But that tenderness didn't deter her, it only made her want for more.

Too bad ranch life and little girls couldn't always wait.

She pressed kisses along his jawline and the prickle of scruff that had grown there overnight. "Time to wake up."

He grunted and pulled her in tighter, his breathing evened out almost instantly as he fell back asleep. She reached her hand down and gripped his morning wood.

His eyes partially opened. "If you were trying to wake me, that's my favorite way, but if you want me out of bed anytime in the next hour or two, that strategy won't work."

"I didn't know how else to get your attention."

Rising up on an elbow, he skimmed his hand across her torso, his broad hand practically spanning her abdomen. He kissed her on the lips but didn't take it any further. "Liar."

"Okay, that wasn't the only way to get your attention, but it was the most fun way."

"Agreed. I promise I'll never complain about you waking me up like that."

Which kind of implied they would be doing this more than once. She liked that idea, even if the execution of it would be difficult since the brutal schedule of the rodeo circuit would conspire to keep them apart.

Before she could allow herself to sink back into him and give the chores on her list a big fat flying *fuck you*, she rolled out of bed.

Sometimes being an adult sucked donkey balls.

She held out her hand to him. "Come on."

He grumbled and groaned but he allowed her to pull him out of bed. "Not even Clementine makes me get up this early."

"Yeah, well we don't want to traumatize her by having her find out her daddy is having sleepovers."

He slipped on his jeans sans underwear and said, "I don't

think her finding me in bed with you would traumatize *her*. More than likely she'd want to join the sleepover which would traumatize *me*."

"Then we're doing the right thing. It would be a sad thing if you could never get it up again." She threw on her robe to run to the bathroom for a quick shower before the day started, knowing she wouldn't be able to concentrate if she had to go the whole day smelling him on her.

He came up behind her, one arm across her chest, the other slipping between the belted folds of her terrycloth robe until he found bare skin. He pressed his erection against her backside. "I think I could find a way to get over it. Might take a lot of one-on-one therapy with a certain kickass, super sexy, stock breeder I know."

She tilted her head back to kiss him because that was her second favorite thing to do with him. "I don't come cheap."

Levi laughed. "I don't doubt that for a second."

He released her and gave her a playful swat on the rump as he gathered the rest of his clothes and swung the door open.

Gramps stopped in the hallway, the smile he'd had on his face dipped, then fell. He glanced between a half-naked Levi and her in her robe. Then to Levi, he said, "Get dressed and meet me outside."

"Yes, sir."

What the hell? That was the same thing her grandfather had said to her prom date—besides the 'get dressed part'—when he'd grilled her date about his intentions with her. "You've got to be kidding me, right? This from the man who comes sneaking in at dawn from the widow Warren's house?"

Gramps' eyes drifted to her for the briefest of seconds before he straightened his shoulders and told Levi, "Five minutes."

After Gramps disappeared inside his room, Olivia turned to Levi. "You don't have to do this. When I decided to stay at the ranch and help with the business, he signed half the ranch over to me. This is as much my ranch as—"

He leaned in and shut her up with a kiss. When he pulled away, he had a hint of a grin on his face. "I'm a big boy, Marsh. I can take care of myself."

"If this is where you tell me to get back in the kitchen and let the menfolk talk, you better rethink that."

He wrapped his arms around her again. "Two of the things I love about you are your fire and your sass."

She glared at him. "Don't patronize me."

"Listing your admirable qualities isn't patronizing."

He went in to kiss her again, but Gramps' door opened. "Two minutes." He stared Levi down as he passed by and stormed out the front door.

Olivia pointed an emphatic finger at Levi. "Don't you dare go out there without me."

"Where are you going?"

"To take the fastest shower ever. I refuse to talk to Gramps when I'm smelling of sex."

He leaned in and whispered in her ear. "I like smelling me on you."

She groaned but refused to admit the same or else they might end up back in her bedroom, and it wouldn't take Gramps any time to find the key to the gun cabinet. Walking backward toward the bathroom, she said, "Wait for me, you got me?"

"Yes, boss."

THE SUN PEAKED OVER THE HORIZON AS LEVI LEANED AGAINST THE porch railing and stared at Olivia's grandfather sitting on the porch swing. "What do you want to know?"

Olivia burst through the screen door, knocking it off one of the rusted hinges.

"I told you to wait for me." Anger had painted her face red, as she aimed her murderous expression at Levi.

Damn, she was beautiful.

"And don't smile at me like that."

Levi held up his hands, happy to surrender. "I'm not smiling," he said through his grin. Her gaze turned even darker. If he survived this conversation with Joe, she was going to kill him.

"And you." She directed her ire at her grandfather, "What do you think you're doing?"

"I want to know his intentions," Joe said. "I'm your grandfather. I have the right—"

"You have no rights where my personal life is concerned. You two can't haggle over me like I'm your prize heifer. Like I'm not even here. This is the seventies, not the thirties. I don't *belong* to anybody. I'm my own woman. I make my own decisions. If I want to have sex before getting married, that's what I'm going to do. If you want to have a conversation about intentions, then you need to talk to me, not him."

"I would tell you to run," Joe said to Levi, with both pride and a touch of amused fear in his eyes, "but by the way you're looking at her, I'm afraid it's too late."

"Yes, sir." Levi didn't have anything to hide. Not from Joe. Not from Olivia. Hadn't he and Olivia gone over this already? Isn't that what being boyfriend and girlfriend meant? That you'd found someone you were crazy about?

"*Arrrrgh.*" Olivia's hands fell to her legs. "I love you, Gramps, but you can be impossible sometimes."

Joe got a sad far off look in his eyes. "You're so much like your grandmother, rest her soul."

"Oh, Gramps." Olivia sighed as she hugged her grandfather over the swing's backrest.

He patted her hand that had come around his neck. His eyes had gone misty, and his voice shuddered when he said, "I'm looking out for my baby girl. You can't fault an old man for that."

"No, I can't." She kissed his cheek then came around and stood beside Levi at the rail. He put his arm behind her back and massaged the tense muscles at the base of her neck. "But this is my life we're talking about. I have a right to be in on the conversation."

"Grampy Joe?" Clementine toddled out of the cockeyed screen door, rubbing the sleep from her eyes.

"Hey, Clem."

"Morning, Pix."

"Did you have a good night's sleep?" Olivia asked.

Clementine nodded and practically sleepwalked to the swing. When the time came, Levi pitied the poor man who would have to deal with Clementine before her morning cup of coffee.

When Joe turned his attention to Clementine, Levi leaned in and whispered in Olivia's ear. "I can't tell you how hot you are when you're on the warpath. Do you think your grandfather would notice if we disappeared into the hayloft for about twenty minutes?"

Her response was a jab to his ribs with her elbow, but he caught the hint of a smile as she turned to her grandfather. With his good arm, Joe helped Clementine onto the swing. She leaned against Joe with her eyes at half-mast.

"What did you want to ask?" Olivia refocused Joe's attention on her. "I've got a bunch of animals to feed before our meeting with the lawyer this morning."

"I just want to know where this thing is going."

Olivia laughed. "We don't even know that, Gramps. This is so new."

Then Joe's eyes bored into his. "Do you like her enough to marry her?"

"Ahhh..." Levi squirmed, not knowing the right answer. Sure, he thought she was amazing. He enjoyed her company, found her smart and sassy and sexy as hell. But marry?

"Don't answer that." To Joe, Olivia said, "It's nothing like that."

Nothing? Sure as hell felt like *something* last night. Even if he wasn't about to pop the question. "It's not nothing. It's something."

She turned to look at him. "Then what is it?"

"I don't know yet, but I want to find out."

With the ongoing conversation, Clementine started to wake from her half-dead state. She climbed onto Joe's lap and started playing with the loose flaps of skin under his neck.

"I don't want you two making any big mistakes." Joe's eyes drifted to Clementine and back to Levi.

"You need to take that back," Olivia said at the same time Levi said, "Clementine is not a *mistake.*"

If Clementine hadn't been in the old man's lap, Levi might have decked the old bastard.

Joe closed his eyes for a slow count of three. When he opened them again, he said, "My apologies. That didn't come out right. Okay?" Joe glanced between Levi and Olivia until they both nodded. "I guess what I'm trying to say is that you're both young and you both have your own responsibilities. You can't let whatever this is between you two get in the way of those things. Marriage is a commitment that takes a lot of thought and introspection. It's not something to rush into."

"We're both fully aware of our responsibilities, Gramps. You and this ranch are the most important things in my life. Clementine is the most important in Levi's. Nothing is going to change that."

"Besides," Levi said, "No one said anything about marriage. Hell, she only now agreed to be my girlfriend."

Joe glanced between the two of them as if he were weighing the truth in their declarations. "Okay then. Glad we got that cleared up. Who wants pancakes?"

Levi groaned as Olivia drove them into town for their meeting with the lawyer. "I think I'm going to be sick."

Olivia glanced over, one hand draped across the top of her steering wheel. "Nervous?"

"It's the pancakes. They're sitting like stones in my stomach."

She laughed. "Maybe you shouldn't have had so many."

"Clementine kept putting them on my plate telling me to eat them. I couldn't tell her no."

"Sure, you could have."

He held his arm over his stomach as the cramping went to critical mass. "You need to pull over."

"What?"

"Pull over now." He reached for the door handle. He'd puke out of an open door while they were moving if he had to, but he wasn't going to throw up on his only suit before going in to see the lawyer.

She stomped on the brakes and skidded to a stop on the graveled shoulder. He tumbled out of his seat and barely made it to the grass before breakfast came back up. He held his tie to his chest to keep it from getting goop-ed up.

He stood there on the side of the road, hands on his bent knees until his stomach stopped heaving. Olivia brought him a rag from the truck and a warm can of soda. "Thanks."

She rubbed his back as he wiped his mouth and took a sip of the drink, swishing and spitting the vile taste from his mouth.

"Better?"

He blew out a deep breath. "Maybe."

With a glance at her watch, she said, "I don't want to rush you, but if you're done here, we need to hit the road. We don't want to be late."

"Yeah, I'm good," Levi lied, his arm still held protectively over his stomach as he crawled back into her truck. He poured the soda out before he closed the door. He had no hope of drinking it and keeping it down.

When she turned into the parking lot of the lawyer's office, his stomach took another violent roll. Okay. So maybe the stomach thing had nothing to do with the pancakes.

Olivia must have picked up on his nervousness because she squeezed his hand. "You've got nothing to worry about. You're a fantastic father, and Clementine is lucky to have you."

"Yeah, tell that to the judge."

"I will, if it comes to that, but it won't. No way the law would ever let June and Clive get their hands on your daughter."

"Man, I hope to hell you're right."

"I am. Let's go. Mr. Reynolds can tell you the same thing."

They were led into an office by a brisk and efficient receptionist. The room was so small, Levi had to let Olivia slide into the chair nearest the wall first, so he could turn sideways in his chair and have room to stretch his legs out past the side of the desk.

When a man walked in, Levi stood to let him squeeze by and stuck out his hand. "Levi Banks. Thanks for seeing us on such short notice."

"Byron Reynolds," the elderly gentleman said. "Joe and I go way back. I'm happy I could get you in."

Then Reynolds turned his attention to Olivia. She stood and gave him a brief hug over the top of the desk. Reynolds said, "Good to see you again, dear."

"Good to see you, too, Mr. Reynolds."

Reynolds sat and folded his hands together on the top of his desk. "What can I do for the two of you?"

Levi dropped the manila envelope on top of the desk and gave the man a brief history about him, Mae, and Clementine, and Clementine's craptastic grandparents.

Reynolds did a lot of nodding and said a lot of 'uh, huhs,' but generally, Levi had no idea how his predicament was playing out. "Well," Levi said when he'd finished. "What do you think?"

Reynolds pulled out the papers and read through them page by page. Levi's knee bobbed up and down while he waited, and Olivia reached for his hand again. Levi held on tight.

Finally, Reynolds set the papers down and took the glasses off the tip of his nose. "I'm not going to lie, this doesn't look good for you."

Bile bubbled up his throat as his stomach did a somersault. Olivia's grip got tighter, and it took him a few seconds to catch his breath. "Why not?"

Reynolds held up his hand and started listing his concerns off one by one. "First, you're a man."

Levi laughed, but it came out biting. "Not much I can do about that."

"Unfortunately, the laws don't favor the father. Especially a single one."

"She's my daughter. I'm the only one she has."

Reynolds held up the papers. "Not according to this. According to this, she has two maternal grandparents who already have an established relationship with your daughter.

Two grandparents who have money and can provide the best things for Clementine. The best schools. The best of everything."

"They can't take her away because I don't have the kind of money that they have."

"The money isn't everything. Though having a job where your income can fluctuate on a whim—"

"Not a whim," Olivia cut in. "It's a hard-won skill."

"That may be, but the suit also lists concerns about your itinerant lifestyle, about the danger to your life inherent to your occupation, about insufficient child care while you're working, about access to schools and education."

The blows kept coming. Levi leaned back in his chair. He hadn't taken this kind of beating in any of the lopsided bar brawls he'd ever been in.

"But that's not the worst of it."

Kapow. The hit came like a kick to the ribs when he was already down and out of the fight. How could the situation get worse than that?

"It says here that you're unfit. That your decisions directly put your daughter's life at risk."

"What the hell are you talking about? My daughter has a roof over her head. Food in her belly. She's happy. She's healthy. Ask the pediatricians I took her to. They'll tell you that's true."

"That's not the concern. The document clearly describes a time when Clementine was in the care of a person, no more than a child herself. A child that—"

"The babysitter was the daughter of a friend and mature for fourteen," Olivia said.

"If that's true, how did Clementine get lost?"

"Shit." Levi rubbed his fingers across his forehead trying to beat back the oncoming migraine. Olivia placed a hand on his shoulder, and he tried to draw strength from her touch. He sat up straighter. "Tell me how we fight this."

Reynolds leaned back and linked his hands across his protruding belly. "You have to do everything you can to make sure the home life you provide your daughter is as stable as you can make it. You need a steady source of income and a suitable living arrangement which doesn't include a camper on a truck."

"No problems there," Olivia said. "He's been hired on at No Bull as our ranch manager and breeding director. Room and board for him and Clementine are included."

"I have?" Levi caught the look Olivia shot him. The one that said don't-be-an-idiot. "I mean, yes, I have."

"That's good," Reynolds said. "You also need a stable relationship. Clementine needs a mother and—"

Olivia grinned. "That's not a problem either, right, honey?"

Honey?

Then Olivia giggled like a school girl, and her eyes got dreamy. He wanted to reach up and put his hand to her forehead to check for a fever. Maybe the pancakes had gotten to her, too. "Levi proposed to me. We're getting married."

Uhhh...

She squeezed his hand.

He cleared his throat. "Married. Yes. Us. Married. Together. Me and her... Yep."

Reynolds stared at him a moment. Levi mentally clapped himself upside his head. Olivia looked like she wanted to do it for real.

"That might help, though our judges are quite conservative. If we could somehow avoid court altogether, that would be our best option."

"Okay." At this point, Levi would agree to about anything, as long as he got to keep his daughter.

"In the meantime, I'll order home visits for you and your

fiancé as well as the Jordans. The evaluation can have a lot of sway with the court if it comes to that."

Levi stood and shook his hand. "Thank you. We appreciate your help. We'll look forward to your call for the home evaluation."

———

"ALL I'M SAYING IS THAT THE NURSE DIDN'T HAVE TO JAM THE javelin in my finger and try to hit the bone," Levi said as he and Olivia trudged down the steps of the doctor's office after receiving their marriage license at the courthouse and getting a blood test to get married.

"It was a little bitty needle. Don't be such a baby."

"Oh, I'm being a baby?"

Olivia laughed. It was the first laugh and the first genuine smile since they'd left the lawyer's office. She may not want to tell him what had upset her—besides the fact she'd agreed to marry him in the hopes that his daughter wouldn't be taken away from him—but he'd get the truth out of her eventually.

"Yes. You're the one who had to look away," he said. "How do you treat your injured animals if you can't stand the sight of blood?"

"That's different."

"If you say so." Instead of turning left to head back to Olivia's truck, he took Olivia's hand and went right.

"Now where are we going?"

"There's a store on the square I wanted to stop by. It won't take long."

They turned the corner and were back at the town square surrounding the courthouse. It was getting close to lunchtime, and the traffic on the square had picked up. People walked the sidewalks, window shopping or getting their errands done.

"We're here." Levi stopped and opened the shop door.

Olivia glanced at the name above the door. "Barrett's Jewelry?"

"Gotta have rings. If we're going to do this thing, we're going to do it right. At least as right as we can."

"We shouldn't waste our money on—"

He laid a quieting finger against her lips. "We're doing this. Period."

With a hand to her lower back, he ushered her into the store. She was the only woman he'd ever met that balked at getting jewelry.

A saleswoman who Levi pegged to be in her forties came out from the back room when she heard the tinkle of the store bell. She'd dressed much younger. Her skirt was short and tight. Her blouse was low-cut and revealing. Maybe the extra cleavage helped with sales.

"Can I help you two?"

"We've come to look at wedding bands."

"Something simple," Olivia added.

The woman's nose scrunched as if Olivia had said a four-letter word, but she recovered quickly enough. "Follow me." She led them to the far corner of the store. "I'm sure we have something you'll love. Sometimes simple can be elegant in its understatement."

He appreciated the way she tried to put a good spin on 'cheap.'

The saleswoman went behind the counter and unlocked one of the glass doors and brought out trays of rings, everything from simple his-and-hers matching gold bands to engagement ring and wedding band sets with undersized solitaire diamonds.

The saleswoman hovered, keeping a close eye on them and the hundreds of dollars' worth of jewelry sitting on the counter as if she were afraid they'd take the lot and run out the door. If they were going to rob the store, they certainly would have gone for the more expensive rings, not the ones that were one step up from the something you'd get out of a bubblegum machine.

"See anything you like?" he asked Olivia.

She picked up the thinnest, plainest set of gold bands, and checked the minuscule price tag. They had to be the cheapest rings in the store. "These are nice, don't you think?"

He appreciated her being thrifty but even though this wedding wasn't real and their budget was modest, in good conscience, he couldn't buy her the cheapest ring at the store. She deserved better than that for her generosity.

Taking the rings from her hand and returning them to the tray, he pointed to another set with wider bands and diamond chips in the engagement ring. "How about these?"

She checked the price.

"Would you stop checking the price?"

She leaned in and whispered in his ear. "I can't afford this ring. I can barely afford the first one we looked at."

What? "You're not paying for your own wedding ring."

"But—"

He saw the rest of the sentence in her eyes—*this isn't real.* "Nuh, uh." Had she really expected him to make her pay for her ring? "I'm paying for the rings. You're the one doing me a favor."

And yeah, maybe that came out louder than it should have.

She kicked him in the shin and gave a curt nod toward the saleswoman who was looking at them a little funny. He straightened and turned up the wattage on his charm. "I mean look at me," he said to the woman. "Who'd want to marry me, right? I'm a lucky, lucky man."

The woman leaned on the counter, her ample breasts one deep breath away from spilling over. "I'd marry you." She reached out and patted his hand. "I've always had a thing for cowboys."

"*Excuse me?*" Olivia said.

The saleswoman stood, having the decency to look a little chagrined. "I was just..."

"Yeah, I'm pretty sure I know what you were *just.*"

The way the heat rushed up Olivia's neck as her anger flared made his heart kick against his sternum and his jeans get tight. She was jealous. Levi smiled.

"We'll take these," Olivia said as if she was suddenly in a hurry to get out of the store. She took the rings he'd chosen out of the tray. "Do you have them in our sizes?"

The saleswoman replaced the trays and locked the cabinet. After taking their ring sizes, she went to check the availability of the rings from the stock in the back.

While they waited, he backed her against the display cabinet, bracing his arms on either side of her. "You're sexy as sin when you're jealous."

"I'm not jealous."

"Says the woman who almost went over the top of the display cabinet to claw the poor lady's eyes out."

"I'm pretty sure if she'd had the opportunity, she'd have dragged you behind the counter and had her way with you."

He leaned in and kissed her like he meant it. Like she was his, even though this whole marriage thing was a farce.

When he pulled away, she opened her eyes and said, "What was that for?"

"For protecting my virtue."

She laughed and gave him a playful swat on the shoulder. "You have no virtue to protect."

How did he get so fortunate to have this amazing woman in his life? One who was willing to marry him, to put her life on hold, to help him keep his kid? He wrapped her in a hug and kissed the crook of her neck. "You're really something special, you know that?"

She shrugged and wouldn't meet his gaze.

"You are. This marriage is a personal risk for you. Divorce is still frowned upon. For women more so than men. What if you fall in love with someone down the road and it's a problem for him that you're divorced?"

The slight smile slipped from her face again. He hated that he was responsible for that, but he wanted to be sure that *she* was sure.

"Then that man's not the one for me."

12

———————

Three days later, Olivia came in from the barn and found Levi on her front porch fixing the screen door she'd busted a few days before. The spring day had heated up fast. It tended to do that in Texas.

Levi had his shirt off and sweat poured down his back. Olivia chalked up her urge to lick every drop off him on the fact they hadn't had sex since that first night when he'd come to the ranch. Even though she'd stood there on that porch and declared to Gramps that she'd damn well have pre-marital sex if she wanted, a small part of her felt weird having pre-marital sex while her grandfather was in the house. But tonight, that would change.

Their marriage wouldn't be real, but it would be legal.

"You don't have to do that," she said. "I'm the one who broke it."

"I don't mind. Besides, I prefer working close to the house while Clementine's napping and I want to keep busy. I'd hate to piss off the boss lady. I've heard rumors she can be a real ball buster."

Olivia rolled her eyes and stepped closer to inspect his work.

147

Not only had he repaired the splintered jamb, but he'd also replaced the rusty hinges and found the roll of new screening and stretched that into place.

"Not bad," she said, "I'll try to remember to put in a good word for you. Maybe you'll get lucky tonight."

Levi groaned. "Please tell me Joe has a date tonight. A very, very, very, late date, because I've got plans for my bride tonight."

"I don't know about a date, but he did say something about wanting the good truck this evening."

"I'm sure if we told him we were getting married this afternoon that he'd be willing to take Clementine for the night. We could splurge on a motel room and everything."

This was sex. This was an *arrangement*. Not a real marriage. She didn't know why he kept trying to make it feel like one. "I don't want him knowing beforehand. I don't think there's any way he could stop us, but I'd rather go ahead and get married, then tell him."

"I think it's a bad idea. What if he wants to be there, what if—"

It was her turn to shut him up with a kiss. Gramps would want to be there for her *real* wedding, but what she and Levi had planned wasn't anything like that. And she didn't want to have an argument with her grandfather before getting married.

Before either one of them could take the kiss any deeper, Gramps came into the den and cleared his throat. They stopped kissing, but Levi left his hand on her hip.

"Don't you look dapper," Olivia said. "Trying to break hearts tonight?"

Gramps pulled the good truck keys off the key holder by the door, the scent of his Aqua Velva aftershave heavy on his skin. Olivia shifted out of the way to let him by.

"Possibly. What about you kids?"

"We've got nothing special planned." Levi dropped the

screwdriver into the toolbox. "Thought we'd hang around the house. I promised Clementine she could have a pony ride on Chunk after her nap."

Gramps shook his head. "You two need to learn to live a little. You need to get out. Kick up your heels. Do something crazy."

Olivia laughed, though it came out strangled. "We'll think about it."

A little more than an hour and a half later, Olivia, Levi, and Clementine stood outside the office of the Justice of the Peace waiting for their turn to marry.

"You remembered the rings, right?" Olivia couldn't get past the feeling that there was something they were forgetting. When you go to get married in a civil ceremony a few short days after making the decision, it wasn't like there was a whole lot of planning involved. Hell, they didn't even have a cake.

Levi patted the front pocket of his best pair of starched and pressed Wranglers. "I've got them, don't worry."

He'd wanted to wear his suit, but she'd suggested jeans, a western shirt, and a sport coat since the nicest dress she owned was a white sundress that hit her mid-thigh. She'd paired the dress with her high-heeled cowgirl boots that she'd kept in a box at the top of her closet for special occasions. She'd figured this qualified.

After all, it wasn't every day a girl got fake married.

"And the marriage license?" Really, why hadn't she thought of this before they'd left the house?

He held open his sport coat, allowing her to see their paperwork peeking out of his inside pocket. He had Clementine in his other arm, her sleepy head against his chest. They'd had to wake her up early from her nap to get her dressed in time for the ceremony.

Stepping closer, Levi rubbed a hand up and down the goosebumps on her arm. "It's not too late to back out. No hard feelings."

Nothing like trying to be talked out of marriage by your fiancé. Olivia blinked a few times, driving back the tears. Could she really go through with this farce and not fall the rest of the way for this man?

Before she could answer, the Justice of the Peace's door opened, and a woman said, "Mr. Banks, Ms. Marsh? The judge can see you now."

Olivia smiled as brightly as she could. "Showtime."

The JP's office was larger than a standard office. It had four chairs aligned two by two on either side of a narrow aisle with barely enough room for the three of them to stand before the judge.

"Will anyone else be joining us?" the JP asked.

The JP wasn't the man she'd expected. Then she'd remembered the elections that past fall. He must have been appointed by the new mayor. The best thing? She didn't know him. Even better, her grandfather probably didn't know him either.

Olivia blew out a breath, and part of the tension between her shoulder blades eased. She had every intention of telling her grandfather about their marriage—it wasn't like it was something they could hide forever—but she didn't want to have to try to rush home and tell him about it before one of her grandfather's old cronies tattled on her.

"No one else is coming," Levi said.

"Have you written your own vows or..."

Like what? To love and to cherish until the custody issue is settled?

"No," Olivia said. "Just say... you know... whatever it is you say."

She glanced at Levi for confirmation. He nodded, though the guilt was clear on his face. He mouthed, "I'm sorry," as if the thought of them writing their own vows hadn't occurred to him.

Olivia offered him a shaky smile. She hadn't thought of it either. She might have taken it as a bad sign, that they weren't meant to last, but this marriage already came stamped with an expiration date.

The JP asked them to join hands. They faced each other, and Levi took her left hand in his right. They couldn't join their other hands because he was holding Clementine.

The JP's voice was no more than a drone in the background. She wasn't paying a bit of attention to anything he said because she was focused on the man and child in front of her—at the way his daughter snuggled beneath his chin, at the way he pressed soft kisses to the top of Clementine's head seemingly without being conscious of it.

As bad as this would be for her heart when the farce ended, she had to do this for them.

Levi squeezed her hand. "That's your cue."

"What?"

Levi grinned. "Say 'I do,' Marsh."

"I do."

The JP said other stuff and then Levi, too, said, "I do." His voice came out gruff, his smile sheepish. She hadn't expected the emotion.

He gazed down at her, surely not with love, but appreciation, affection, and a whole lot of lust.

"You may kiss your bride."

Levi wrapped their joined hands around his back, drawing her in, his kiss warm and gentle yet detached as if he were going through the motions the way they had been for the past ten minutes.

Then he pulled away a fraction before coming back for another. This time, when their lips touched, she heard the groan, felt the need licking around the edges, the desire—leashed and bound—struggling to break free.

Her hand went to his belt buckle before she realized what she was doing. The JP cleared his throat, and Olivia tried to pull away. Levi stopped her with an arm around her neck and whispered in her ear, "I love that you've done this for me. For us. Thank you."

His sincerity, his sentiment made her chest tight and the emotion bubble up and catch in her throat. However wrong this was, it also felt so right. He pressed a kiss to the top of her head and set her free. She swiped at the errant tear before anyone could notice.

"A kiss for the camera," the JP's assistant said.

They turned to find the woman at the end of the short aisle with a Polaroid camera in her hand. The kissing and hugging had jostled Clementine awake. Levi switched Clementine to his other arm, so she'd be between them, then they each pressed a kiss on each side of his daughter's cheek as the camera clicked and whirred.

The lady pulled the photo free and waved it around to help it air dry. She handed it to Levi, and the three of them watched their image appear out of nowhere.

Kind of like their marriage.

————

LEVI CAME DOWN THE HALLWAY AFTER PUTTING CLEMENTINE DOWN for the night. "I'm really sorry about dinner."

Olivia sat at the kitchen table with a stack of bills, the ranch's checkbook, and a bowl of melting chocolate ice cream she'd hardly touched.

She hadn't even heard him.

He pulled up a chair and snatched the pen from her hand.

"Hey, I was using that."

"Olivia Banks." He liked the way that sounded a little too much. "You're not paying bills on our wedding night."

"It's not a real—"

He made a sound to shut her up, that same sound he always used on Chunk when his gelding tried to kick at his stall. "If you say this isn't a real marriage one more time, I'll—"

"You'll what?" At least she was smiling now, her emotions had been up and down since they'd said their "I do's."

"I don't know yet. I'll think of something though." Then he slid the marriage certificate across the table to her. The one signed by them, the JP, and the JP's assistant, who'd acted as their witness. "This is as real as it gets, Liv. You're my wife. I'm your husband. Period."

"Until we're not."

"If this is going to work, if we're going to show a united front for the home evaluation and the custody hearing, if we want to prove that we can provide a stable environment for Clementine, we have to be able to sell this marriage to the town, to the court evaluators, to everyone. And to do that, we have to believe in it ourselves."

She blew out a breath and sat back. "Which means we have to live it every day. Like we're really newlyweds, like we're really, hopelessly, madly, insanely, in love."

He picked up her hand and kissed her palm. "Now you're talking, Mrs. Banks."

He scooted his chair out farther and dragged her onto his lap, wrapping his arms around her waist. "I really am sorry about dinner."

"It was fine. Pizza is never a bad choice."

"Not for beer night with the boys, but for your wedding night? No way. I should have stopped in at the grocery store and bought Clementine a snack to hold her over until we could get real food."

"I appreciate the thought, but she wouldn't have been able to sit still that long at The Bistro, the line was out the door, and their service is slow. It would have taken an hour to be seated."

"We really don't deserve you, but on behalf of my daughter and I, I'm so infinitely glad you're ours."

Olivia hugged his head to her chest, and with his nose buried in her cleavage, suddenly he didn't feel so bad any more. She'd pulled her hair back into a ponytail after they'd arrived home, but she still wore the same dress she'd worn to the JP, and he couldn't wait to get her out of it.

He skimmed his hand beneath the hem of her dress, and up her thigh. She tilted his head up, working her kisses along his jawline until she came to the pounding pulse beneath his jaw. She shifted, her ass pressing against his erection.

He hooked a finger into the front of her dress. The material stretched, and he pulled the fabric down lower, exposing a nipple to the play of his thumb as he nipped and sucked the curve of her breast. Her back arched and she guided his mouth to her nipple.

"*Mmmm*," she muttered, the sound so low, so deep, it resonated in his body, heating his veins. "I think this marriage needs to be consummated. You know, for appearance's sake."

He scooped her up into his arms. "I like the way you think, woman."

They'd almost made it to the hallway before Olivia said, "Wait, wait, go back."

Levi stopped. "You're kidding me, right?"

She had one arm around his neck, but she made a paddling motion with her free hand like he was a canoe and she could muscle her way back to the kitchen.

He returned to the table, and she reached out and grabbed the bowl of ice cream. When he lifted a questioning brow at her, she said, "Trust me, you're going to like this."

Levi wasn't convinced but he was game for whatever. He bypassed her room with the partially opened door and took Olivia to the guest room. She shoved the door closed with her foot.

"You put Clementine in my room?"

He set Olivia on her feet and the bowl of melty ice cream on the nightstand. "This bed's bigger."

And he planned to use every extra square inch of it.

By his calculation, it was his turn to sit on the bed and watch her strip. He sat up against the headboard and used the same words she'd used on him a few days before. "You first."

She grinned, the kind of devious grin people get when they are up to no good. It tantalized and delightfully terrified him at the same time. He kicked off his boots and scooted farther up the bed.

Toeing out of her boots, she hiked her dress up to her hips and slowly worked her panties down her legs, allowing only teasing glimpses of her sex.

She shot her panties at him like a slingshot, and he caught them, the crotch damp in his hand. "You need to hurry."

Instead of stripping off her dress, she reached over and turned off the bedside lamp, pitching them into near darkness. In the corner of the room where Clementine's cot had been, the night light remained on, its faint amber glow barely enough light to see Olivia's silhouette.

"Why'd you do that?"

"Just wait." Olivia shimmied out of the dress, a maddening inch or two out of reach.

"I need to get my hands on you."

"Ah, ah, ah. Hands behind your head."

He groused but did what she'd asked, his dick knocking hard at his zipper.

"Do you have a condom on you?"

"Nightstand," he said, proud of himself that he'd remembered to move the rubbers into the room after he'd put Clementine to bed.

She retrieved one from the drawer and opened the packet. Levi loved how she got one ready before they got started. He'd had many friends who'd taken unnecessary chances and gone without because they didn't want to take those extra seconds to put one on in the heat of the moment.

Hell, he'd been one of those idiots with Mae.

Sitting on the edge of the bed, she slid his jeans and underwear to his knees, restricting his movement, then she went for his shirt and worked her hands between the snaps and yanked. The snaps gave with a wave of *pop, pop, pop, pop.*

"Oh, yeah," she said. The slow swipe of her tongue through his belly button made his dick dance.

He clasped his hands behind his head. His fingertips tingled with the need to touch her. She ran her hands up his chest and then tucked the tails of his shirt behind him.

"I can't move. You've got me hog tied." Which, to his surprise, only made him harder and the need to bury himself inside her that much greater.

"That's the point." She nipped at his chin. "You ready?"

There was only one correct response for that. "Oh, hell, yeah."

She climbed onto the bed, straddling his hips, trapping his cock flat against his abdomen beneath her. Then she leaned across him, reaching for the ice cream bowl.

"What do you think you're doing?"

The swish of the spoon as she stirred the soupy ice cream in the bowl provided his answer. Starting high on his chest, she ever so slowly dripped the chocolate onto his chest using long, broad strokes like an abstract artist. She scooped up more, aiming for one of his nipples.

Drip.

Drip.

Drop.

His nipples pebbled beneath the cold. Goosebumps flashed across his chest, down his arms, and shot up to the top of his skull. Then the tortuous trail of chocolate continued down his sternum, filling his belly button. He'd never be able to eat ice cream again without getting a hard-on.

The mental image of what was to come, of her tongue licking her way down his body, slurping up the ice cream, eased a groan from deep within. He ground up against her, her wetness soaking him.

Then she sat up straighter and dropped one final dollop on the head of his cock. He couldn't keep his hands behind his head any longer. He expected her to complain, but she only laughed.

Gripping her hips, he ground against her, loving the friction, the pressure, and the slick slide of their bodies together.

She replaced the bowl on the nightstand. "Oops. I guess I'd better clean up my mess."

When she went to start at his chest, he said, "You need to start lower."

She scooted back, her weight on his thighs, and licked his dick clean. "Good God almighty, woman." The talented things she could do with her tongue. "I'm pretty sure I heard angels sing."

Her throaty laughter around his cock made the base of his spine tingle. He reached for the condom and managed to free himself long enough to put it on.

"You don't like it?" A sly smile played on her lips, knowing damn well the effect she was having on him. The proof was in her hand.

"I like. Too much."

Then he lifted her, and she reached between them and took him in her hand, guiding him into place, a throaty groan escaping her as she slid down to his balls. *"Daaamn,"* she said with a reverence and awe that made his muscles quiver and his balls go tight with this burning need to drive into her.

He kicked off his jeans, freeing his legs. Wrapping his arms around her, he hugged her against his torso, the ice cream slipping, sliding, and sticking between them. She kissed him then. She tasted of creamy, rich chocolate and pure unadulterated sass.

Rolling, he reversed their positions.

"You got me sticky and messy." By the delicious way her voice dipped, it was a turn on, not a complaint.

"Sorry, not sorry." He raised up on his forearms, their bodies peeling away where they'd stuck together.

With his tongue, he worked one chocolate covered nipped then the other as he increased the force and speed of his thrusts. Her hands went to his ass encouraging him to go faster. Rising on his haunches, he wrapped his arms around her thighs and pounded into her, her breaths coming short and quick.

She reached one hand to the apex of her thighs, stroking herself as he felt the first blinding pulse of his orgasm. "Just like that, baby," he said.

Her body stiffened, and her stroking slacked off as her internal muscles clamped down around him, sending him flying, his nerves pinging, and his heart stampeding in his chest.

"That was... epic." Her chest rose and fell as she caught her breath.

"Mmmm." He licked a spot of ice cream from between her breasts and wrapped her in his arms, his own breath ragged, raw. "I think chocolate is my new favorite flavor of ice cream." He pulled out, rolling onto his back and taking her with him.

"I second that." Her voice had that sexy, sated purr she got after she'd been fucked. It was almost enough to get him aroused again. "We've got a problem though." She didn't sound too worried.

He lazily trailed his fingers up and down the small of her back. "What's that?"

"We'll have to think of another grounds for divorce besides impotence."

He grinned, feeling stupidly happy, even though getting it up had never been a worry. "You sure about that?"

She rose up on an elbow. "Fairly. I may require a larger sample size. I only have tonight and the other day as data points. They could have been one-offs."

Giving her ass cheek a squeeze, he said, "Give me a few minutes and a shower, and we can work on increasing the sample size."

13

———

THE THING ABOUT RUNNING A RANCH AND HAVING A THREE-YEAR-old in the house was that sleeping in amounted to a luxury. One that, even the day after her wedding, Olivia couldn't allow herself to indulge in. She had a young heifer due to give birth any minute that she needed to keep a close eye on as well as her other chores to attend to, and then there was Levi, who had Clementine to deal with.

That's why she found herself in her robe in the kitchen making coffee before the sun came up, despite the fact Levi had added two more data points to her sample size. Who would have thought Olivia would have become such a fan of empirical data?

Between her legs sat a delicious rawness of which she could also become quite enamored. A gentle warm breeze blew through the window above the kitchen sink. It wouldn't be long before the days grew too stifling and she'd have that same old argument with her grandfather about having central air conditioning installed in the house. He figured he'd survived the last seven decades without it, he could survive a couple more.

The chug of her grandfather's diesel engine got louder as he came home after a long night out. The truck door slammed, but

160

he caught the screen door as he entered the house before it whacked the jamb and woke Clementine.

Gramps shuffled into the kitchen as Olivia poured him a steaming cup of joe. She glanced at him over her shoulder. There were bags under his eyes, his hair lay slightly disheveled on his head, and a private smile deepened the laugh lines on his weather-worn face.

"You're looking a little rough," Olivia said. "I'm not sure a cat would have been brave enough to drag you in."

With his sling long forgotten, her grandfather braced his hands on the counter with a clack as his cast hit the solid surface. He dropped his head between his shoulders as if it were taking every bit of his strength to stay vertical.

"What's the matter? The widow Warren start taking her vitamins again?"

"Elenore."

"What's that?"

He glanced up at her, his smile gone. "The widow Warren has a name. It's Elenore."

"I know. I didn't mean... I just..."

Gramps glanced up at her then, his once brilliant blue eyes had faded to near silver, but they were as sharp as they'd ever been. "Do you have a problem with me dating again? It's been years since your grandmother passed..."

She tried hard to school her expression. Who was she to judge what her grandfather did or who he dated? He had as much right to full autonomy and his own personal life as she'd asked of him for herself.

"You disapprove."

"It's not that. I'm happy for you. For both of you. Grandma would be, too. She would never want you to be alone. But calling Elenore by her name makes the reality of grandma being gone seem much less abstract."

"I get it." Her grandfather's his normally calm, steady voice chipped and cracked at the brittle edges. "I miss her, too."

"I meant no disrespect."

"It's okay, baby girl." Her grandfather pulled her into a hug so tight it made her ribs sore, her heart squeeze, and her eyes threaten to leak.

With a pat on the back, they finally parted. He rubbed the moisture from his eyes with his thumb and forefinger. "You going to hand me that coffee or are you going to make an old man beg?"

He took the proffered mug from her hand and caught her wrist, looking pointedly her wedding band. "I think you have explaining to do, missy."

"It's not like that."

"I'm old. I'm not blind." Gramps took a sip of his coffee, leveling a be-straight-with-me stare over the top of his mug. "So, the sneaking around, the sleeping in his room, and the slipping out the next morning is nothing?"

"Exactly."

At least to Levi, it was nothing. Their marriage was nothing but a piece of paper. A means to an end.

"But the two of you got married."

Olivia broke free from his grasp and poured herself a cup of coffee. This wasn't a conversation she'd looked forward to, and she refused to do it decaffeinated. "It's not real."

Sure as hell felt real last night when Levi had been balls deep, and you'd called out his name. Oh, and that damn ache between your legs? That's certainly real.

Physically real and emotionally real were two entirely different things. Sure, they were attracted to each other and the sex was the best she'd ever had, but enchanting, exhilarating, intoxicating climactic sex didn't make a marriage of convenience any less of a transaction just because their genitals had no complaints.

"You're going to get yourself hurt."

"I'm not." At least she hoped not. "We both knew what this was going into it. I owe it to Mae."

"You don't owe her this. It's too much. She never would have asked it of you."

"Then I owe it to a little girl who's already lost too much. This isn't a forever kind of deal. When the custody hearing is over, we can quietly file for divorce and go our separate ways. Lord knows I don't need to be saddled with more responsibility at this time in my life."

If a part of you hadn't craved the responsibility and, more importantly, the connection, why did you suggest the marriage to begin with?

Olivia ignored her inner voice. What did it know anyway?

If she'd placated her grandfather, she couldn't tell from the frank disapproval on his face.

"You don't have to like it," she added. "But you do have to live with it. At least for the time being. You think you can do that?"

Gramps harrumphed. Hard to tell if that was a yes or a no, but Olivia didn't push. He'd come around. He always did.

From behind her, Levi cleared his throat as he came into the kitchen and beelined it for the coffee pot. He was already dressed, ready for a full day of work.

"Morning," Olivia said.

Levi cut his eyes at her false cheer as a deep groove formed between his brows, his answer little more than a grunt.

Not your typical morning-after-marriage-and-night-of-hot-sex kind of greeting. Oh, God. Levi was *pissed*. Or hurt, or... hell, she didn't know how to read that sour expression. "So how much of that did you hear?"

"Enough." He refused to look at her.

"I can explain. Gramps, can you give us a minute?"

Levi's mug hit the counter with enough force to shatter, but her grandmother's old mugs were made of sterner stuff. "No need for explanation. Everything you said was true." He plucked his hat off the hat rack by the back door, leaving his coffee untouched. With her grandfather's limited ability to work with his broken arm, her grandfather had taken to watching Clementine when he was home. To Gramps, Levi said, "If you could bring Clementine to me when she's up, I'll take her off your hands."

Levi's eyes raked both of them. "Now if you'll both excuse me, I've got work to do."

"Levi, wait." But he didn't. *Shit.*

"Give him a few minutes to cool off. Then go to him," Gramps said. "I've got Clem."

She kissed him on the cheek. "Thanks, Gramps."

After a little searching, Olivia found Levi out by the tractors, wrestling with a tread-worn tire that couldn't hold pressure for more than a few hours at a time, which made doing any kind of tractor work twelve times harder.

She would have done it herself, but the enormous tire was too heavy for her to take it in for repairs. And she'd refused to ask her grandfather for help. He didn't need to be trying to lift heavy things at his age.

"Can we talk?" she asked.

"I think you've said enough."

What should have taken two strong men to lift, Levi manhandled into the pickup by what looked like sheer force of will from the energy he'd generated from the steam billowing out of his ears.

He turned toward the driver's side of the truck, but she put her hand on his arm, stilling him. "Levi."

He refused to look at her when he said, "I think it's best that we don't confuse what this marriage is with anything else that might be going on between us. We can continue the charade in town, but I'll move myself and Clementine back into the guest room."

"I can have sex with you without catching feelings, if that's what you're worried about. You're a big boy, Banks. I'm sure you can, too."

"That's all this was to you? Scratching that itch?"

"Is it not?" Why did her damn heart pause that beat waiting for his denial? The denial that never came.

———

It was late on a Thursday afternoon, a day shy of their two-week anniversary. And just as long since he'd had his hands on his wife. Was it any wonder he'd been grumpy and on edge the entire time?

Like most spring afternoons in Texas, the day had warmed up quickly. Levi pulled a bottle of beer out of Olivia's fridge and popped the top. Though grateful Clementine was still down for her afternoon nap, he should wake her if he ever wanted her to get back to sleep before midnight. But with the court-ordered evaluation coming after dinner, he'd take these few quiet moments for himself.

He stepped out onto the porch and sat on the swing in the cool shade. The cardinals chirped and flitted around as an easy breeze kicked up. Across from him, Chunk grazed in his paddock, his normally tight and tucked up belly already starting to protrude with so much time off. Between taking care of Clementine and working on the ranch, Levi hadn't even had a chance to saddle his horse and go for a ride.

But Chunk's burgeoning hay belly was the least of his concerns with the evaluation on the horizon. He'd be lying if he said it didn't feel like the beginning of the end. Not that he wouldn't fight and keep on fighting until there was no question Clementine was where she belonged. With him. But good lawyers were expensive, and Clive and June had the means to keep fighting for custody long after he went bankrupt.

He took a long drag of his beer, quenching his thirst, but the alcohol did nothing to ease the tension knotting up the muscles between his shoulder blades. When Olivia returned after a quick run into town to get supplies, those muscles of his twisted tighter.

He should have gone with her, but he'd used Clementine's need for a nap as his excuse even though that kid of his could have fallen asleep in the truck and never woken up until they'd gotten home. He knew that. What was worse was Olivia knew it, too.

To be honest, Levi had needed that physical and emotional space after two weeks of working side by side with Olivia and not being able to touch her or kiss or take her to his bed.

He hadn't felt that alone or disconnected since... since, well, ever.

And he couldn't stand the thought of driving into town one more time with his kid and Olivia and their fake-ass marriage and their manufactured public displays of affection trying to sell what they had together as real.

That first Saturday morning after the greatest night of his life, when Olivia had told him she was perfectly capable of having sex with him without catching feelings, had been a boot heel to his heart. The problem was, he'd already caught feelings for her—big, bad, scary, hairy feelings with long claws that had dug deep beneath his skin and refused to let go.

Even if he wanted to make a serious go of their marriage, he couldn't unhear Olivia's unguarded words in the kitchen with her grandfather. That the last thing she wanted or needed was more responsibility.

And she'd been right. Clementine was *his* responsibility, not hers.

Olivia climbed out of her truck looking like she needed the beer more than he did. When she reached into the bed of the truck, he said, "Leave it. I'll get it in a minute."

"I got groceries and—"

"It can wait a minute. Come sit. I'll get you a beer." He turned and walked back into the house, not giving her a chance to refuse.

She was sitting on the swing when he returned. She took the bottle from his hand and patted the seat beside her. His thigh brushed hers as he sat.

He scooted over, breaking the contact. "Sorry."

"You don't have to apologize for touching me. Not after what we've done to and for each other."

Her cheeks pinked as if she too were remembering the places he'd had his hands, his lips, his tongue. His jeans got uncomfortably tight, and it took everything he had not to reach for her and drag her across his lap.

Circling the lip of her bottle with her finger, she said, "I miss it."

With his forearms draped across his thighs, his half-drunk beer dangling from his fingers between his legs, he gently pushed the swing back and forth. He was almost afraid to ask what she was referring to, but he was too tired for anything but honesty. "What's that?"

"Your touch."

Sitting back, he met her gaze, expecting that fun, flirtatious, turn of her lips, and that naughty glint in her eyes he'd come to miss much more than he probably should. This time, what met him was this striking openness and perhaps a touch of shock at admitting so much of the truth.

"I—" He took a long swallow of beer, trying to ease the stricture in his throat and loosen the words that had become a stacked-up jumble of letters that didn't make sense anymore. But like her, he was tired of tip-toeing around the obvious. "I can't touch you without wanting you. I can't want you without wanting, not just the sex, but wanting it all—the sex, the touch, the intimacy, the emotion, the *connection*. I'm not wired for the casual, at least not with you I'm not."

Olivia glanced away. "*Shit*."

That boot heel she'd planted square in the middle of his heart left a bruise that twinged with every beat. "Forget I said anything, I don't—"

"It's not that," Olivia said, pointing at the cloud of dust rising above the ranch's long drive. "She's here. The court evaluator. She's early."

14

"Why is she so early?" Sheer panic etched Levi's face. "She was supposed to come after dinner."

Olivia didn't have an answer for him, though she considered it more of a rhetorical question.

He shoved his beer into her hand. "Take those inside. I'll wait for her out here."

"There's nothing wrong with having a beer."

"I know," he said, "but I don't want to make a bad impression."

She shifted the bottles to one hand and for reasons she wasn't quite ready to acknowledge rose up on her toes and touched her lips to his. With a hand on his cheek, she said, "You can't help but make a good impression. She's gonna love you."

The way you do?

Just because she missed his touch, missed their late-night talks, missed the man who had quickly become her best friend, didn't mean she loved him.

Then what the hell does it mean?

He gave a quick toss of his head toward the screen door, the expression on his face begging her to make the alcohol disappear. She left the porch as the silver four-door sedan pulled up next to her truck.

In the kitchen, she poured the beer down the drain and listened as Levi introduced himself. The spring on the screen door squeaked, and then the frame bumped against the door jamb.

"Sweetheart." Levi used his most sincere-sounding, loving-husband tone. "I want you to meet Betty Higgins."

Olivia rinsed and dried her hands and met them in the entryway, offering her hand. "Nice to meet you."

Betty Higgins smiled, but it was one of those polite smiles screwed into place by someone who'd rather be doing anything but smiling. The woman was probably in her late fifties, with a dowdy wardrobe and a dour face.

Levi hitched a thumb over his shoulder toward the bedrooms. "I'll get Clementine up from her nap—"

"Isn't it a little late for her to be napping?" If Betty had been wearing pearls, she probably would have clutched them in horror. Maybe Betty was June's long-lost twin sister. Betty glanced at her watch as if making a mental note about the time.

"One of the heifers gave birth last night, and Clementine wanted to see—" Levi cut himself off.

Betty's lips went flat and grim as if Levi had just told the woman he'd taken his three-year-old out for a hedonistic night of drinking and drugs.

Good thing Olivia had dumped their beers like Levi had asked. Heaven forbid this lady find out they had dared to have a drink before five o'clock like uncivilized heathens.

"Let her sleep," Betty finally said. "We have things to discuss first."

Levi lead them to the kitchen table, pulling out a chair for Betty and one for Olivia. He took the seat in between the two.

"Can I get you something to drink? Water? Coffee? Sweet

tea?" Olivia offered, only remembering then that she'd left the ingredients for the chocolate chip cookies she had planned to make in the bed of the truck. But she wasn't going to leave Levi even for the short time it would take her to bring the groceries in.

"Sweet tea, please."

While Olivia got their refreshments, Ms. Higgins went over Clive and June's case for custody. When Olivia set the three sweet teas on the table, Levi thanked her, but by the dyspeptic expression on his face, if he tried to drink anything, there was a good likelihood it wouldn't stay down.

"As you can see, most of the Jordans' concerns are irrelevant at this point," Levi said. Only someone as familiar with him as Olivia was would catch the tension in his voice. "I have a steady job. A wife. A stable home life for Clementine. A great elementary school in town for her to go to when the time comes. I assure you, my daughter is happy and well adjusted."

"Speaking of the marriage. The timing—"

"There's nothing wrong with the timing," Levi insisted. He locked eyes with Olivia and said, "I love her. That's what matters."

Olivia swallowed. Hard. When he said it like that, with that intensity, with that sincerity, Betty would almost have to believe him. Olivia knew better, and still he'd almost convinced her.

"Lebi?" Clementine's sleepy voice came from down the hall as she hugged the door jamb still dressed in the dirty clothes she'd worn to the barn that morning.

Levi jumped out of his seat, the chair legs making a barking sound against the wood floor. "Hey, Pix. Let's get you changed, and you can come meet the nice lady who came to see you."

Olivia knew that he'd had plans to have her bathed and dressed in her favorite pink dress by the time Ms. Higgins showed up, but it was a little too late for that now. Levi disappeared down the hall, and Olivia turned to Ms. Higgins and said, "He's really good with her."

"She calls her father by his first name?" The shock and horror had returned to the woman's face. She'd probably get positively apoplectic if she ever found out Levi had, on occasion, allowed Clementine to have dessert before dinner.

"Clementine knew him as Levi first. She knows he's her father. He didn't want to force her to call him daddy before she was ready."

"Dr. Spock says in his book on child-rearing, that—"

"Levi's read the book. We both have."

Ms. Higgins clucked and washed her disapproval down with a swallow of sweet tea. Hopefully, all that sugar would help make the woman less sour.

Levi returned with a sleepy Clementine in his arms as she clutched her doll. The doll's one eye never got unstuck, so she had a permanent wink. Olivia thought it was cute. Levi thought it was creepy.

Levi had changed Clementine into the pink dress and wrangled her unruly hair into two lopsided pigtails, a smudge of dirt still on one of her cheeks.

"What I still don't understand," Ms. Higgins said, "is why the child's mother never told you that you were her father."

Levi turned Clementine in his lap, so she could play with her doll on the table. "I wish I knew. I would have stepped up. I did step up when I found out. I should get points for that at least."

"Mr. Banks, this isn't a game where the one with the most points gets the prize. Or in this case, your daughter."

"I know that. Clearly."

How Levi maintained his cool, Olivia didn't know. As it was, her temper needle climbed into the red zone. This woman had come into their home with her preconceived ideas of what made good parents, and nothing the woman said gave Olivia any confidence that she saw a man who'd do everything in his power to keep his daughter in his life.

———

CLEMENTINE GIGGLED AS LEVI BOUNCED HER ON HIS KNEE, ONLY HE wasn't doing it to keep his daughter entertained, he was doing it because he couldn't catch a break with the evaluator and it was his only acceptable outlet for his nervousness and his spiking anger. He figured wrapping his hands around the woman's scrawny neck wouldn't win him any points.

Not that points mattered, according to Betty Higgins.

But Levi couldn't see how they didn't. With every question, with every disapproving turn of the evaluator's lips, every suspicious raised brow was like another chalk mark in the never-give-this-man-custody column. It was like the last seconds of the final quarter, the bottom of the ninth with two outs and two strikes, the buzzer as the football spirals toward two defenders in the end zone of a double overtime game... And they were losing.

Losing to a man and a woman who'd driven their own daughter to drugs.

Five minutes into Ms. Higgins' indulgent soliloquy of the Jordans' virtues as the perfect guardians for Clementine, Olivia interrupted. "You do know that Mae's wish—Clementine's mother's wish—was for her daughter to stay as far away from the Jordans as possible."

"I don't believe the wishes of a drug addict should hold merit. Especially where a young child's welfare is concerned."

Levi slammed his palm down on the table, his untouched glass of tea jumped, and the amber liquid spilled over the top. Clementine went quiet. Olivia reached under the table and squeezed his thigh. Ms. Higgins' eyes rounded, and she glanced over her shoulder as if looking for her best route of escape.

But Levi had had enough.

"Who the hell do you think drove Mae to drugs?" Levi stood, placing Clementine on the ground so he could dispel a fraction of his pent-up rage by pacing instead of putting his fist through a wall.

"Mr. Banks, if you'll sit down—"

But he couldn't sit. He paced to the hall and back again. "Who do you think destroyed Mae's self-confidence? Who do you think diminished her day in and day out until drugs were her only way to cope with the hurt and pain? I don't know what the Jordans told you to make you swallow their heaping pile of bullshit, what kind of farce they put on, but I refuse to let them raise my kid, and to poison my kid into thinking she's not good enough."

"Bull*shit*. Bull*shit*," Clementine sing-songed as she galloped one of her toy horses around her doll.

Ms. Higgins' face blanched, but Levi wasn't finished yet. He jabbed the table with his index finger for emphasis, ignoring the way Clementine had turned cuss words into a children's ditty. "I want my daughter to know every day that she's good enough. That she is *everything*. No one will love her the way we do."

Ms. Higgins gaped. Levi thought he might have to toss the tea into her face to re-engage her brain, but figured he'd probably done enough damage for one night. He picked up Clementine and held a hand out to the door, inviting the evaluator to leave. "I think we're done here."

"I'll see you out." Olivia stood, and the look she gave Levi was a cross between what-the-hell-have-you-done and atta-boy.

Olivia waited on the porch until the car started and the sound of the engine and tires on the gravel died in the distance. He stood Clementine on the table noticed the smudge of dirt on his daughter's cheek. Had that been there the whole time? He licked his thumb and went to clean it off, then stopped himself. His daughter didn't have to look perfect. More importantly, she didn't have to *be* perfect.

He set his daughter on the ground again, dirt smudge and all, as she ran to her toys. Behind him, he heard the screen door close. He was too afraid to turn around and look at Olivia.

She came up behind him, threading her arms around his chest and hugging him from behind. It was their first significant contact since their wedding night. He covered her hands with his and closed his eyes. Keeping his voice low so his daughter wouldn't overhear, he said, "I really fucked it up, didn't I?"

She pressed a kiss to the knot of muscles between his shoulder blades. "It could have been worse."

"I don't see how. What she saw was a short-tempered man who can't keep from cussing in front of an impressionable kid."

Olivia didn't say anything.

To prove his point, he added, "Did you see the color drain from her face when I slapped the table? I've never seen snow that white before."

"It wasn't that bad."

He scoffed.

"Unless she was blind, she also saw a man devoted to his daughter, a man who changed his life to make his daughter's better. That's no small thing."

"Maybe. But is it enough?" He turned in her arms, and she clasped her hands behind his waist.

"We'll have to wait and see. Don't forget, Ms. Higgins' recommendation is only one of the criteria the judge will base his decision on. Your lawyer said that even if she recommends the Jordans get custody doesn't mean the judge will grant it."

"But Reynolds said it's rare the judge goes against the evaluator's recommendation."

"Rare. Not non-existent. "

They spent the rest of the evening cooking dinner after which the three of them made the cookies that they'd planned to make for Betty Higgins. They did their best to ignore the ax dangling over their heads by playing with Clementine, checking on the new-born calf, and tucking Clementine into bed an hour past her bedtime.

As Levi read her a short story, he couldn't help but wonder if these sweet nights with his daughter were numbered.

Levi left Clementine's door ajar, allowing some light from the hallway to spill in. He leaned against the wall outside her room and scrubbed his hands down his face, his stubble course beneath his fingers. Hell, he hadn't even had a chance to shave. No matter. There wasn't much he could have done to make his impression worse on the court evaluator. A little stubble was the least of his worries.

Olivia came out of the restroom and he caught her hand as she walked by. She stopped, and said, "Are you okay?"

He shook his head. At that moment, he was probably the farthest from being okay as he'd ever been in his life. Forget the broken hearts, the failed relationships, the career lows, the financial struggles, the bumps and bruises, and broken bones. None of that compared to that precise moment when he realized there was a good chance—no, scratch that—a great chance that Clementine could be taken away from him.

Whatever personal problems he and Olivia were having, he pushed those aside. Giving her hand a light tug, Olivia willingly stepped between his legs, and he wrapped his arms around her shoulders and pulled her in tight. His face went to the crook of her neck, as he breathed in her scent, that magical mix of wonder and woman that he couldn't seem to get enough of.

He didn't know how long they stood there taking and giving strength to each other. Long enough for their breathing to match, and their hearts to beat in time. Olivia leaned back a fraction and asked, "Nervous?"

"No." He took a deep breath. "Scared shitless."

Levi cupped her face, rubbing his thumb along the bottom edge of her lip. He ducked his head a fraction, waiting for her to back away or tell him to stop. When she did neither, he dipped his lips to hers, brushing, tasting, daring.

He mentally kicked himself for allowing the rift between them to continue for so long. And for what? Pride? Ego? He broke the kiss and waited for her eyes to open.

"What are you doing?" she asked.

"Kissing my wife." His *wife*. He liked the way the word *wife* rolled off his tongue.

"*Nuh uh*," she said, her voice teasing, but he couldn't miss the undercurrent of seriousness in her tone. "You check out for two weeks, you don't get to call me that."

"I've caught feelings." There. He said it. With the custody hearing looming, he had less tolerance for the gargantuan elephant sitting in the middle of the room. Might as well kick it in the ass and see what happened.

"I haven't."

"I don't believe you."

Olivia dropped her forehead to his chest, shaking her head before glancing back up at him, the exasperation stamped on her face. "You know, I was right all along. You are a cocky asshole."

Levi grinned for the first time that day. Maybe for the first time that week. Something about that sass of hers really gassed up his engines. "Doesn't make me wrong."

———

It had been three weeks since the court ordered evaluation, but they'd had plenty of work to occupy their time.

Olivia looked down at the newborn calf she'd helped pull from her best breeding cow. This was the calf she'd been waiting for. The matchup between her best cow and one of the industry's top bucking bulls.

Blood and amniotic fluid still covered the calf's brindle coat. It wasn't breathing. With a towel, Olivia quickly cleared the calf's nose and mouth of fluid. The mother lay on her sternum, too exhausted to even turn her head and look at her calf, much less try to lick it clean.

Levi grabbed handfuls of clean straw and stood over the calf, rubbing it down and trying to stimulate it to breathe. "Come on, little one. You can do it."

While Levi worked on the calf, Olivia clipped and cut the umbilical cord, then helped the exhausted cow deliver the afterbirth.

"How is it doing?" Olivia asked.

As if in answer, the calf coughed, and coughed again, then took one shuddering breath, and then another. Levi dropped to his knees, turning the calf over and stimulating the calf from the other side. "Coming around."

From her spot behind the cow, Olivia crawled over, checking the calf's gums. As it took a few deep breaths, the blue-tinged mucous membranes lost that dusty hue and turned pink. Olivia sighed and sat down in the shavings, her back to the stall wall. "What is it? Boy or a girl?"

Levi lifted a rear leg and grinned. "Looks like No Bull has a possible future contender for rodeo's next top bucking bull."

"Holy cow," Olivia said, not oblivious to the pun. "Jettison did it. He finally sired a son."

"Not bad for an old bull who's mostly shooting blanks now."

"No kidding. I think Jett's breeding days are over, but hopefully, we can get a few more years out of him on the circuit."

"For an old bull, he's still one of the best. I can count on one hand the number of bull riders who made it to the buzzer."

"Having Silas Foss and Tobias Navarro off the circuit has certainly helped Jett's ranking. Those two were part of a select few to have ever figured him out."

"And if this bull is anything like his sire, it will keep No Bull's reputation at the top of the roughstock industry."

Olivia rubbed the stray hair off her cheek with her shoulder, probably the only area on her that was clean. "I sure as hell hope so. This ranch could really use the break."

"Ollie, Lebi." Clementine skipped into the barn, skidding to a stop at the open stall door. "Oh, a widdle baby. I wanna see."

Joe caught Clementine's hand before she could run into the stall. "Hold up, Clem. You can't run in there. The momma won't like that."

"But Lebi—"

"Listen to your grampy, Pix."

"*Awh.*" Clementine plopped on her butt and crossed her arms over her little chest, her bottom lip sticking out.

Levi had to fight back his grin. He stood and washed his hands in the bucket of warm water in the corner of the stall.

Joe said, "There's a phone call for you, Levi. It's Byron Reynolds."

The levity dropped from Levi's face, the tension immediately returning. It seemed like every time a little joy came into their lives, they got another reminder that this cozy little family dynamic they'd settled into these last three weeks was essentially nothing more than a mirage.

Levi swallowed hard, then cleared his throat. "What did he want?"

"Didn't think it was my place to ask."

Levi reached down, tucked Clementine against his hip, and pressed a kiss to her temple. Olivia almost offered to keep Clementine while he talked on the phone, but it looked like he needed his daughter close for the time being. He walked away without another word, his big shoulders slumped under the heavy weight bearing down on him. It wasn't just the world sitting on his shoulders, it was his whole universe.

"You two doing okay?" Gramps asked.

"Sure." Olivia moved the calf closer to its momma's head so the cow could finish the cleaning job Levi had started. Then she went to the bucket and washed up.

"Look at me, baby girl." Gramps leaned a shoulder against the stall, the compassion in the soft lines and wrinkles on his face threatened to bring tears to her eyes.

She blinked them back. A fat lot of good tears ever did. "Dammit."

Her grandfather's voice dropped. "Come here."

Olivia stepped over and he held her against his chest, oblivious to the muck on her clothes. "This is what I was afraid of. You're gonna get yourself hurt."

"That doesn't matter." Her voice came out muffled against his chest. "The only thing that matters right now is making sure Clementine stays where she belongs."

"That's bullshit, and you know it."

Olivia pulled back.

"You matter as much is that little girl does." Then he sighed, and added, "Sometimes your heart is too big for its own good."

The tears came, and she swiped them away one by one. "Don't worry. This will be over soon enough. Levi will get custody, they'll go back to the circuit, and our lives will get back to normal."

Her grandfather rubbed his hands up and down her arms. "Is that really what you want?"

She laughed, but it came out sounding wet and congested. Those damn tears. "Doesn't matter what I want. He can't stay here."

"Come again? I thought this was working out well. We needed the extra hand, and he's doing a fantastic job. He's hard-working, responsible, and more importantly, I think he has real feelings for you. But maybe that's the sentimental old man in me. Tell me I'm wrong."

Olivia rubbed her eyes, then watched as the calf tried to stand on shaky legs. The cow heaved herself to her feet with a grunt, and Olivia closed the stall door. She couldn't look her grandfather in the eye when she said, "So he says."

"Then what's the problem?"

"He's only here because he has to be. He works hard because that's the kind of man he is. But his heart isn't in it. It's out there, on the road, on the back of his horse, chasing the next rodeo, and the next one after that. As much as I would like him to stay, I can't ask that of him."

"Why the hell not? Seems to me he's asked a lot from you."

"That's different." She reopened the stall and removed the water bucket before it got knocked over.

Her grandfather didn't say anything until she turned and looked at him. His bushy, gray-peppered brows were raised in that way that demanded a satisfactory answer. She'd always caved to that brow while growing up. It didn't matter that she was an adult now, it still held power over her.

"He's not happy here. I am. If I asked him to stay, he just might. And he'd make the best of it, for as long as he could. But he wouldn't be able to do it forever. Eventually, being here would wear him down. And I don't want him to resent me for asking that of him."

"There's more to life than the circuit. There's home. There's family. There's the love of a good woman. That's more than any man has a right to ask for."

"Maybe, but it took you many, many years to realize that yourself. You can't expect a man in the prime of his career to drop everything and get there overnight."

15

<hr>

BY THE TIME LEVI HAD HUNG UP THE PHONE WITH HIS LAWYER, JOE was back inside the house and getting Clementine changed for a trip into town. Levi and Olivia still had a lot of work to do to get ready to bring a replacement bull to the Santa Fe rodeo for the upcoming weekend.

Which was for the best. After his talk with his lawyer, Levi knew the decision that had been rolling around in his mind had to be made and made now if he was ever going to have a chance of keeping custody of Clementine.

He went outside to find Olivia hooking up the stock trailer to the newer truck. He finished directing her as she backed up to the hitch, then lowered the hitch onto the ball. "That's it, we're good."

Olivia mashed her foot on the parking brake and cut the engine, while Levi attached the chains and the trailer lights.

"What did Reynolds have to say? Good news?" Olivia leaned against the tailgate.

"Maybe. He subpoenaed the records of the rehab facility and the psychiatric ward Mae had been in after her previous suicide attempt."

"What do Mae's medical records have to do with anything?"

"Maybe nothing. But Reynolds hopes that maybe he can find something in there, something the psychologists had found, or maybe something Mae had told them that might help the judge understand that Clive and June aren't fit to be Clementine's guardians."

The bad news? The news he couldn't bring himself to tell Olivia? As good of a lawyer as Reynolds was, he didn't come cheap. His time, his investigation had already eaten up the retainer Levi had given him, and he was running on credit. Reynolds was a good man and was willing to work with Levi on the fees, but he didn't work for free. Levi needed to come up with more money. Fast.

"That sounds promising, right?"

"It's a start."

"Did you decide which bull you're going to send to Santa Fe to replace Toot Sweet?"

"Jettison's the only one available. At least of the caliber they need for Santa Fe. He's rested up. He should give the boys a good run for their money."

Levi grinned. "I know a lot of bull riders who will be cursing your name."

Olivia laughed. She hadn't done enough of that lately. And he blamed himself for that.

"I'm good with that." Then she looked at him. Really looked at him. "What is it?"

"I have a favor to ask you. One that I have no right to ask. You've already done so much for me."

"You're my husband. You're allowed to ask me for favors." Then she stepped closer and wrapped her arms around his neck. Her voice dropped, when she said, "Especially after that... um... *favor* you did for me last night."

Levi groaned and snugged her up against him. "I don't think

it can be considered a favor when I enjoyed it as much as you did."

"Still..."

Levi pressed his forehead to hers. "Let me take Jettison to Santa Fe." When Olivia looked at him with open curiosity on her face, he added, "I know you'd prefer to stay here anyway. I thought I'd leave Clementine here, if that's okay with you?"

"Of course. But what aren't you telling me?"

Levi both loved and hated the easy way she read him. "I have things there I need to take care of."

"Things?"

"I'll tell you about it. When the time comes." He hated being so cryptic, but if Olivia knew what he'd planned on doing, she'd try to talk him out of it. And the worst part was, he kind of wanted her to.

But at this time in his life, what he *had* to do wasn't the same thing as what he *wanted* to do. But right now, his daughter mattered most.

It had grown dark by the time Levi had packed, and they'd loaded Jettison into the trailer. He said his goodbyes to Clementine, then took his suitcase and threw it into the tail bed.

Olivia followed him out of the house. "Be careful on the road. Stop when you get tired. It's a long drive, but it's not worth pushing it. Promise me you'll stop and get a motel if you get too tired."

Levi leaned against the truck and pulled her between his thighs. "I promise." He brushed her hair out of her face, her skin soft beneath his hands. He leaned in, brushing his lips to hers. He wanted to drag her back into the guest room, crawl under the sheets with her, and not come up for air until morning.

They hadn't spent a night apart in the last three weeks, and he'd come to look forward to their time alone each night. He was gonna miss that. Miss her. Miss *them*.

And of course, he'd miss Clementine. But that's why he had to go. He had lawyer's fees stacking up that he had to pay.

"You should go now," he said. "You know how Joe gets if you let the supper he cooked get cold."

"You should stay. At least long enough to get dinner."

"I can grab something on the road. Don't worry about me." He gave her a pat on the ass and said, "Go on, now."

She started backing up. "Call me when you get there. I don't care what time it is."

"I will." Levi climbed into the truck and waited for her to disappear inside the house before he loaded his horse in the trailer behind the bull. He grabbed his saddle and the rest of his tack and tossed it into the pickup. Selling his tack and the best horse he'd ever owned wasn't something he'd ever thought he would do, but with his kid's future at stake, what kind of choice did he have?

———

AFTER DRIVING THROUGH THE NIGHT AND MOST OF THE NEXT DAY with only a few stops along the way to fuel up and water and feed the animals, Levi finally arrived at the Santa Fe rodeo grounds. It was Thursday afternoon, and the grounds were beginning to fill up with arriving competitors.

Muscles and joints complained as he climbed stiffly out of the truck. He rubbed the sleep from his eyes and trudged to the rodeo office to find a pay phone. He dreaded calling Olivia, not because he didn't want to talk to her, but no doubt she'd discovered Chunk was no longer at the ranch. Selling his horse would hurt like hell, and he still didn't trust her not to try to talk him out of it.

He dropped coins into the pay phone and dialed the ranch's number. After a few rings, Olivia picked up.

"It's me."

There came an audible sigh over the line. "You made it?"

"Yeah. Hey, I don't have a lot of time to talk right now. I still need to find Rusty, get Jettison off the trailer and taken care of, and find a place to crash for a few hours."

"How's Chunk?"

He loved how she got right to the point and called him on his bullshit. Still didn't mean he wanted to talk about it. "He's good. Look I—"

"Why didn't you tell me you were taking him?" Her words held more curiosity than accusation. And perhaps a little hurt. It wasn't that he didn't trust her, it was that he didn't trust himself not to go through with selling his horse.

"I don't know," he hedged. He had to clear his throat when it unexpectedly got tight. Damn. Selling Chunk was gonna be even harder than he'd expected. Unlike some competitors Levi knew, his horse wasn't a means to an end. He'd raised him from a foal and put the time, the energy, the training, and the heart into making one of the finest bulldogging horses in the industry. More than that, Chunk was his friend. But now he had to choose between his horse and his daughter. It wasn't Chunk's fault that it wasn't even a fair contest. "Tell Clementine I love her and miss her."

He used to enjoy the long days and nights on the road going from town to town, from rodeo to rodeo, event to event. For the first time, after less than twenty-four hours on the road, he truly felt alone. He wanted to tell Olivia that he loved and missed her, too. But the words wouldn't come. Probably for the best.

Their divorce was already going to be a bitch.

"I'll tell her."

The line buzzed and cracked as the silence dragged on. He didn't want to hang up. Apparently, neither did she. Levi rested his forehead against the metal box surrounding the pay phone, listening to her breathe.

Finally, she said, "And Levi?"

"Yeah, boss?"

"Take care of yourself."

Say it. Tell her you love her. He opened his mouth but saying those words wasn't something he wanted to do over the phone. That was something he wanted to do in person. Especially for the first time. "You too."

After he hung up, he went to the concession stand and bought a large, much-needed cup of coffee. A hand clamped down on his shoulder, and Levi startled, the hot coffee spilling over his hand.

"Oh, shit. I'm sorry, man."

Levi shifted his coffee to his other hand and shook off the hot liquid. Turning, he found Tobias Navarro behind him. Toby had been one of the circuit's top bull riders who'd almost had the life stomped out of him last summer by a bull so dangerous that many people thought it had no business being on the circuit. Levi and Toby had never been especially close, but they'd thrown back a few beers together in their time.

Levi wiped the spilled coffee onto his jeans and stuck his hand out. "Hey, Toby. It's been a while."

"Too long. Though any time away from the circuit seems too long. You know what I mean?"

"Tell me about it," Levi said, even though for the first time, it didn't feel like the truth. "You here for fun?"

"The best kind. The doctors finally cleared me to compete again." Toby didn't quite meet Levi's eyes when he said it.

"That's great. No one expected you back for at least a few more months."

Toby got a sheepish smile on his face. "Yeah, well..."

Levi narrowed his eyes at Toby. "Those doctors didn't really clear you, did they?"

"You know how doctors are. If I'd listened to everything the doctors said, I'd have been elected president of the knitting club years ago."

"I hear you." Levi really needed to see to the animals and catch a nap. He stuck out his hand again. "Good luck out there this weekend."

"Thanks, man."

Levi searched the stock pens behind the main arena and found Rusty filling a water trough for a pen of steers. He was quick to help Levi unload Jettison and Chunk and get them settled in for the night.

Afterward, Levi declined an invitation for a few beers at the bar and headed over to one of the side arenas where several of his old bulldogging buddies had been practicing their runs. But by the time he got there, the place was nearly deserted except for Cooter Craw and a young kid that had started bulldogging professionally earlier that year.

"Well, I'll be," Cooter said when Levi walked up to them. They exchanged handshakes and a one-armed hug. "How's that daughter of yours?"

"She's great, thanks for asking." It felt strange that he didn't have Clementine's little hand in his or have to worry about keeping a close eye on her. It had become the norm so quickly that not having Clementine there made him feel out of sorts.

"Levi." The kid tipped his hat. The kid had the best of everything. Top of the line boots and hat, a shiny new truck and trailer, and a dad willing to finance his kid through the circuit. The only thing the kid didn't have was a top-notch horse.

"Jonas." Levi clasped the kid's hand. "Just the man I wanted to see."

"Oh, yeah?"

"I'm going to dinner." Cooter clucked and tugged on his horse's reins. "See you two later."

They said their goodbyes, and then Jonas said, "What can I do for you?"

"That offer you made me for Chunk a while back—"

"You mean that time when you laughed in my face and told me not only no, but hell no?"

Levi pushed his hat back farther on his head and returned Jonas' smile. "That would be the time. You still interested?"

It was Jonas' turn to laugh in Levi's face. It came off high pitched. Jesus. Had the kid even hit puberty yet? "You're kidding me, right?"

The smile slipped from Levi's face. "I wish the hell I was, kid."

Tall and lanky, Jonas crossed his arms over his narrow chest. Levi didn't see how the kid could wrestle steers to the ground without snapping his toothpick arms in two. "Why do you wanna sell?"

Levi wasn't getting into his personal life with a kid barely out of diapers. "If you don't want him, say so. I'm sure any one of your competitors would love to have him."

That Jonas was probably the only one, thanks to daddy's money, who could afford to pay what Chunk was worth, was hopefully lost on him. Jonas really didn't have to worry that the competition would buy Chunk out from under him, but the kid didn't know that, and Levi wasn't idiot enough to tell him.

"I'm interested. We could saddle him up right now and—"

"Naw," Levi said, "I hauled him over from Texas. Let's give him the night to rest." Then Levi had an idea. "I tell you what. If you're seriously interested, you can use him on your run tomorrow night. Let you see for yourself how he is when the money is on the line."

Jonas' wide smile exposed gaps between his front teeth you could drive a double-decker cattle trailer through. "How much?"

"You compete with him. Then we'll talk numbers."

"You got yourself a deal." Jonas' grin was genuine.

Levi's fell flat and short, and there was this biting feeling in the pit of his stomach as if a rat were trying to gnaw his way out. He should have been thrilled he had someone interested in Chunk, not feeling queasy.

———

Sunday night after the bulldogging finals, Jonas and his father met Levi at Chunk's stall. Jonas held onto Chunk's reins as Jonas' father counted hundred-dollar bills into Levi's hand.

Chunk slept on the end of his reins, oblivious to the transaction that would change his circumstances.

Levi tucked the bills into his wallet and said, "If he doesn't work out for you, you call me, okay? You don't sell him on to anyone else."

"No, sir," Jonas promised. "You get rights of first refusal if I ever want to sell him. But I'm telling you, after tonight's run, that ain't gonna happen."

Jonas' father clapped his son on the shoulder. "Between the horse and those pointers, you gave Jonas, he's really got potential. I can see it."

Having a personal best was far from winning checks, but the kid had the drive, the ambition, and that spark that said he wouldn't stop until he made it to the top. Now what the kid needed was more muscle and experience. Both of which would come with time.

"Think about what I said for the offseason." Jonas' father shook Levi's hand. "I'd love to send Jonas to you for a few weeks of one-on-one instruction if you can spare the time."

"I'll keep it in mind." Levi reached up and ran his fingers through Chunk's forelock, his gelding's...no. *Jonas'* gelding's eyes opened half-mast, that lazy, after-competition-haze having settled in. He hugged that big, blocky head to his chest and whispered in Chunk's ear. "I'm sorry, buddy."

Levi gave a wane smile to Jonas and his father and turned on his heel before he could throw the money back at them, load his horse in the trailer, and find another way to pay his lawyer's fees.

But there wasn't another way, so Levi kept walking.

He wandered aimlessly around the concourse until it was time for the bull riding. He caught up with Ian around the chutes. Levi climbed onto the top of the empty chute beside his friend.

Ian took one look at Levi and said, "I was going to ask if you'd sold Chunk already, but one look at your face and I know the answer."

"And here I thought I was hiding it so well."

"I'm sorry, man. If Cora and I had any money—"

"Don't," Levi said. "I appreciate it. I really do. But this is my problem. And Chunk's just a horse, right?" Levi's voice cracked, and suddenly he didn't sound so tough.

"Sure." By Ian's tone, he didn't believe it for one second either.

Someone wolf-whistled, catching Levi and Ian's attention. Ian put his camera to his eye and started snapping. From under the concourse came a tall redhead decked out in her chaps and hat with a bull rope slung over her shoulder.

"Hey beautiful, if you want something to ride, I'm right here," a bull rider Levi hadn't seen before said.

The woman kept walking toward the first chute—the one Jettison had been loaded into—ignoring the idiot's comments.

"Who the hell is that?" Levi asked.

"Belle Brock. The circuit's newest bull rider."

"No shit?"

"You can't make this stuff up. But hey, more power to her. I guess the rodeo commission—with a little help of a lawsuit—has decided she has as much right to be stomped into the dirt by the bulls as the next guy."

"That woman's gotta have a heavy set of balls."

"That ain't even the half of it. The bulls aren't what she has to worry about. It's those assholes who don't think she belongs there."

One of those assholes jumped down from one of the chutes and landed in front of her.

She stopped. "If you'll excuse me."

"Not so fast, lady."

"I've got a ride."

"Not until after you pay the toll."

"And what would that be?" She managed to maintain a bored expression, even as a second guy jumped down from the chutes behind her, effectively blocking her in. If they frightened her, she didn't show it. Levi shifted, ready to jump into the mix if need be.

"A kiss," the asshole said, to a chorus of whoops and catcalls.

"A kiss." She pushed up the brim of her black Resistol hat as if giving the 'toll' due consideration. She crooked her finger at him, and he took a step closer. She put her hands on his shoulder and said, "Close your eyes."

The whistles got louder, and everyone laughed. Everyone except Toby over by the first chute. He looked like he was about to leap across the top of the rails and murder the guy. The asshole closed his eyes and puckered his lips. With her hands on his shoulders for leverage, Belle Brock drove her knee into the asshole's nuts, dropping him in a fresh, wet, pile of manure.

The whistles and cheers stopped. Belle glanced around from

face to face to face of her competitors. "Anyone else like me to pay a toll?"

The asshole still lay on the ground, cupping his balls and gasping for air, his friends shook their heads, the shock keeping their tongues in their head.

Toby grinned, looking thunderstruck.

Belle stepped over the downed man. Toby steadied her arm as she climbed up the chute onto Jettison's back. Maybe the old bull had met his match.

The bull riders certainly had.

Turns out, Levi had been wrong about Jettison. The old bull hadn't lost his touch, and Belle lasted less than two seconds before flying through the air and landing hard enough to have the wind knocked out of her.

The crowd in the stands went deathly quiet, and the other bull riders climbed to the top rail watching with concern. When she finally caught her breath and stood, the crowd cheered and stomped their feet as if she'd made the eight seconds on the champion bull.

Levi had to hand it to her. If he'd drawn Jettison for *his* first professional ride, he might have backed out. Levi didn't stick around for the rest of the bull riding. He had an early start in the morning hauling Jettison and Toot Sweet back to the ranch.

The next morning, after a fitful night of restless sleep, Levi had that same urgency to get on the road he always had the morning after a rodeo had ended, only this time he wasn't looking forward to the next city, he was looking forward to getting home.

Home.

He hadn't had a place he could call home since he left for the circuit the day after graduating high school.

Home.

Where he had a roof over his head, a beautiful wife, an

amazing kid, and a job that, while he didn't love it, he could find a certain satisfaction in a hard day's work.

His goal had always been to get back on the circuit after winning custody, but the rodeo that had always fit him like his favorite pair of well-washed jeans, now itched and scratched and chaffed.

And even *if* he wanted to go back to bulldogging... He didn't have a horse.

Holy Hell. What the devil had he done?

16

Levi met up with Rusty at the fairgrounds to load Jettison and Toots Sweet. Jim Thomas and Bob Forney were busy loading No Bull's other stock onto trailers to take them to the next rodeo. Most of the competitors had left the night before.

Earlier that morning, Levi had walked past Chunk's stall to give him one last pat, but the stall had already been stripped bare, his horse long gone.

Probably for the best.

With his trailer loaded, Levi said his goodbyes and started pulling out. Off to his left, one of the guys who ran the pony ride was behind his trailer whipping the hindquarters of a small pony trying to get it to load into an already overcrowded trailer.

Levi threw his truck into park and stormed out, slamming his driver's door. The man stopped whipping the horse long enough to glance up.

"You need help?" Levi asked, even though what he really wanted to do was yank that whip out the man's hand and put a few red stripes across the idiot's back to see how he liked it.

"The little shit won't get in. It's always like this. But I always win in the end."

Levi didn't know what it was that made him reach into his back pocket for his wallet. Maybe it was because the pony had the same stocky build and color as Chunk, even down to the white star on his forehead, or maybe it was the raised welts on the horse's rump, or the ribs that stood out like bars on a jail cell, or the long hooves that had turned up at the toes like elf slippers from lack of care, or the big, brown eyes that looked at him for help. Maybe it was all those things. But Levi wasn't leaving the rodeo grounds without that pony.

"How much?"

"He ain't for sale."

The man raised the whip again, but Levi caught the man's wrist before the lash could rain down on the horse's hide. Levi squeezed until the whip dropped from the man's hands with a clatter. "I'll ask you again. How much?"

The man's knees buckled under the awkward angle Levi had twisted the man's wrist. "*Owh*... Damn, man... Okay, okay. Two hundred bucks."

Levi laughed but dropped the man's wrist. "I'll give you twenty-five. You'd be lucky to get that from a kill buyer, and you know it."

"Seventy-five."

"Fifty, and you throw in that beat-up excuse for a kid's saddle."

The man grumbled, but said, "I ain't helping you get that little shit into your trailer."

As if Levi wanted this man's help. Levi counted out the cash, stuffed it in the guy's shirt pocket, and took the pony's lead rope in one hand and the tiny saddle in the other. By the time Levi made it back to his truck and stowed the saddle, the man was long gone.

The pony didn't look like he'd have the strength to stand in the trailer and ride the entire way back, so Levi stuffed hay into a hay net and tied it inside the trailer, then spread out a flake on the floorboards so the pony could lay down if he wanted to. When it was time to load, Levi clucked twice, and the horse hopped in as if he knew better times lay ahead.

Levi secured the lead rope, giving the horse enough slack to lay down if it needed, but not enough to get himself tangled, then closed the trailer and started on his long drive home, feeling for the first time that weekend that he'd done something right.

———

OLIVIA HAD JUST SAT DOWN AT THE KITCHEN TABLE WITH HER lunch when she heard the chug of a diesel engine roll past the house. She jumped up and hurried to the door. Levi. She'd pictured this the whole weekend, how she'd stand in the open doorway, and wait for him to come to her, but somehow that's not what happened. In reality, she found herself taking the porch steps two at a time and hitting the dirt at a run.

Turns out, almost a week away was about six days too many.

He made it out of the cab and she leaped into his arms. He laughed, his arms coming around her and holding her tight. "You miss me?"

She would have answered, but she'd already pulled him in for a kiss. Taking, tasting, devouring. She dropped her legs and slid down his body as he took the kiss deeper. He backed her against the tail bed, one hand sneaking beneath the hem of her shirt, as he straddled her leg. His fingers found bare flesh. She broke the kiss, closed her eyes, and savored his touch.

"Where's Clementine and Joe?"

Olivia opened her eyes. Even in the midday sun, Levi's eyes went dark and needy.

"Joe and Eleanor took Clementine to the park to play with kids. I'm expecting them back any minute."

Levi nibbled his way up her neck, and whispered in her ear, "After almost a week away, a minute is probably all I need."

The trailer shook, and one of the bulls let loose a long, low, bellow. Olivia said, "I think someone's ready to get off the trailer."

For a brief second, Levi buried his nose in the crook of her neck, and breathed in deep, before slowly backing away. "I've got a little surprise."

"Oh yeah?"

Levi took her hand, and she allowed him to pull her to the trailer door. It took a second for what she saw to register—a small chestnut pony, not Chunk. "Where's your horse?"

Levi started undoing the trailer door latches, busying himself with offloading the animals instead of making eye contact. He untied the pony's rope and led the poor animal out of the trailer. It was immediately obvious the animal had been neglected and abused.

"*Levi.*" She caught his arm and forced him to turn and look at her. "Where's Chunk?"

"I sold him to an up-and-coming kid."

"*What?* I thought you'd taken him to compete."

"I needed guaranteed money. A lot of it."

Olivia knew he wouldn't have sold Chunk unless he thought he didn't have any other options. And after the call she'd taken from his lawyer that morning, she knew he'd also done what he'd had to do. But that couldn't have made it any easier.

"And this little guy?" Olivia stuck her hand out, and the pony nuzzled her fingers.

"He belonged to one of those pony ride guys. The guy was a certifiable dick, and I thought after a bit of quality care, the pony would be a good choice for Clementine." His laugh stumbled and fell. "If I even have custody after this is said and done."

"You *will* win," Olivia said it like she believed it. Because the alternative wasn't an option any one of them could live with.

"God, I hope you're right."

"Come on. We can put this little guy in one of the birthing stalls with the paddock out back until he settles in."

They had released the pony into the stall with fresh hay and water when Olivia told Levi about the call from his lawyer. "Reynolds called this morning. Good news, I think. He wants us to meet with him first thing in the morning. He says he's cautiously optimistic we might be able to avoid a court hearing."

"No shit?" Levi looked too tired and worn to dare hope. "Did he say how?"

"No. He seemed pretty hush-hush about it. But there was an excitement in his voice that he couldn't hide."

A horn honked, and Olivia and Levi came out of the barn to find Clementine running toward them. "Daddy, daddy!"

Levi scooped Clementine up and swung her around, her peals of laughter infectious. "What did you call me, Pix?"

Instead of answering, Clementine wrapped her little arms around his neck and buried her face against his chest. Olivia pointed at Levi and asked Clementine, "Who is this?"

"Daddy!"

"Oh, baby," Levi said, his voice unnaturally thick, "I missed you."

With his free arm, he wrapped it around Olivia's shoulders and pulled her up against him, his lips pressing against her temple. When he released her, he was quick to wipe his eyes.

"I told you it was only a matter of time," Olivia said. From day one, Levi had shown Clementine nothing but love, compassion, loyalty. He deserved this one small victory. Olivia smiled, but couldn't help but think how devastated they would be if Reynolds was wrong.

———

OLIVIA WAS LEANING UP AGAINST THE HEADBOARD AND READING the latest edition of *Farm and Ranch Magazine.* It was an interesting article on hay crop fertilization schedules that she found intriguing until Levi entered the room, a towel slung low around his waist, his hair damp and dripping on his chest. Olivia's mouth went dry while another part of her got incredibly wet.

She'd be lying if she said she hadn't been looking forward to this moment all evening. Okay, okay. All week. Anticipation made her hands shake, and the pages of the magazine rattle. She dropped her eyes back down to the article, feigning disinterest. "Clementine asleep?"

Olivia turned another page. She read the next sentence three times, but she still didn't know what it said. The door lock clicked. Levi's towel hit the floor with a muffled thump. Olivia's mouth started salivating. *Sweet Jesus.*

The edge of the bed dipped, and Olivia chanced a glance over the top of her magazine. Levi was on his hands and knees at the foot of the bed, stalking his way toward her. He snatched the magazine out of her hands and tossed it on the floor.

"Hey, I was reading that."

Levi crawled closer, his large hands resting on either side of her hips. He leaned forward, his mouth, inches from hers. His smile grew when he said, "Not anymore."

He wrapped an arm around her waist and scooted her down onto her back until he could straddle her. He glanced at the T-shirt she wore, and mock glared at her. "Hey, that's my shirt. I want it back."

"Now?"

"Now."

"Really?"

"I must insist." He grabbed onto the hem and pulled it over her head, his eyes dropping to her breasts.

"Satisfied?"

He leaned in and dragged his tongue over one taut nipple, and then the other. "I plan to be. Along with you."

"You've got a lot of lost time to make up for, cowboy."

"I'm pretty sure I'm up to the task." He eased back and started kissing his way down her chest, a hand roaming across her belly before trailing a teasing finger down the inside of her thigh. As much as she wanted the slow tease, she also wanted a quick, hard-pounding release.

Heat and heaviness settled at her core, and she reached into the bedside table for a condom. She tore the corner with her teeth, and said, "I need you now."

He took the condom from her hand and quickly sheathed himself. Shifting positions, he settled between her thighs, his weight on his forearms. He kissed her on the lips, his mouth opening hers, his tongue diving in.

This is what she'd wanted, what she'd been waiting for. How could she have gone from wanting a no-strings fling to needing and wanting the strings and knots and entanglements that a life together would bring?

Her tongue danced with his. She reached between them and took him in her hand, enjoying the thick, heavy weight of him. Guiding him to her entrance, she dared to say, "I missed this. Missed *you*."

"*Mmmmpff*—" his word became mangled as he slid into her inch by glorious inch. When he'd filled her, he paused, and his forehead dropped to her chest. His breath caught. "I missed you, too."

He kissed her. It wasn't with the hard, demanding strokes of his tongue that she loved and had become accustomed to. This kiss held a soul-piercing tenderness that she'd never expected from him.

Slowly, he began moving inside her, not the quick hard thrusts of a desperate need and passion, but a nuanced and controlled giving and taking. A sharing of their bodies, of their experience, of their want and need for each other. He took her hands in his, linking their fingers, and holding them above her head, his slow, sensuous thrusts rocking her gently.

"Look at me." When she did, he said, "There you are."

She found it hard to hold his gaze. The depth of the raw emotion she saw in his eyes was both sinfully sweet and exquisitely painful. He stilled inside her, drawing more of her attention. "I love how you've been there for me. I love the selfless way you've sacrificed for me."

He kissed her cheek, her chin. "I love how we fit together, how we can laugh, how we can fight, how we can make up."

His lips pressed against the pounding pulse at the base of her neck.

"I love how I miss you when we're apart, and I love how you love me when we're together. But most of all, Olivia Marsh, *I love you.*"

Her heart squeezed, and her chest refused to draw in air as he resumed the long, languid strokes. He'd effectively said he'd loved her before, but that was with an audience, that was when he was playing a part. But this was different. There were no court evaluators in the room. No judges, no lawyers, no acquaintances on the street. Just the two of them. He didn't have to say those words unless he meant them.

His breath got ragged while he waited for her response, the pulse thrumming in his neck as he stroked in and out of her. She didn't know what their future held. But whatever they had to face, she wanted to face it with him.

She freed her hands to cup his face. "I love you, too, Levi. I don't want a divorce."

His eyes closed, and a slow smile spread across his face. When he opened them again, he said, "Good thing. After I pay this next round of lawyer's fees, I don't think I could afford to give you one anyway."

"*Hey*, you promised," Olivia teased. "We haven't even made the two-month mark, and you're already breaking your promises to me."

"How about I make you a new promise? One I can keep."

"What..."

His thrusts got harder, faster, and as her orgasm built, and the tingling in her nerves increased, Olivia had a hard time forming words, much less complex thoughts and sentences.

Levi chuckled and bit at her earlobe. "I promise to always be there for you, to always love you, to always put our family first. "

As his strokes got erratic, and his breath blew hot against her skin, she knew that was a promise he would keep.

17

―――――

Levi hadn't been able to eat a bite of breakfast before the meeting with Reynolds but he sure as hell wanted a swig or two or more of whiskey. Something, *anything* to calm that gnawing in the pit of his stomach, that hopelessness eating away at his soul.

He and Olivia were sitting in Reynolds' claustrophobic office waiting for Reynolds to arrive. Levi glanced down at his and Olivia's joined hands, her knuckles had gone white. Shit. He loosened his grip and rubbed the circulation back into her hand. "Sorry, babe."

She kissed him on the cheek. "It's fine. I'm a lot harder to break than that."

"What the hell is taking him so long? We've been waiting—"

"Five minutes. We've been waiting five minutes. And we were fifteen minutes early. It's okay. Every thing's gonna be okay."

He looked at her then. While he appreciated the support and her optimism, it fell flat to his ears. "You don't know that."

"I don't. But assuming the worst isn't going to help matters."

Maybe she was right. Though he couldn't bear to get his hopes up, only to have them dashed. It would break him.

There came a knock on the door, and Reynolds' secretary poked her head in and said, "If you'll follow me, please."

Levi extricated himself from his chair and pulled Olivia along behind him. "Where are you taking us?"

"The conference room." The secretary led them down a back hall and knocked twice on a door labeled 'conference room' before opening it. She motioned them inside. "Mr. Reynolds will be in shortly."

Levi was brought up short in the doorway when he saw June, Clive, and another suited man Levi assumed was their lawyer already sitting at the table. "What the hell is going on here?"

"That's what we'd like to know," the suit said. The man stood and offered his hand to Levi. "Dick Norris. You must be Levi Banks. And your girlfriend?"

"My wife, Olivia Banks."

Norris spared Olivia a short nod. June gave a derisive snort that said *wife, my ass.*

Before Levi's tongue and temper could get the better of him, Reynolds walked in and took a seat at the head of the table. Levi settled across from Norris, Olivia across from June, and Clive was seated to June's left.

Reynolds had left the door open, which Levi thought odd, but it wasn't like the lawyer's office bustled with activity. They were likely the only clients there at the time.

Norris pointedly looked at his watch. "If you don't mind, Mr. Reynolds, I have to be in court in an hour."

Reynolds straightened the manila folder on the table. "Certainly. We wouldn't want to keep you." He pulled a document from the folder and slid it to Norris. "As soon as your clients sign this, everyone can get on with the day."

Reynolds' tone, while courteous, held a hint of triumph.

Olivia squeezed Levi's hand. He was afraid to breathe. Norris eyed Reynolds for several long seconds before glancing down at the document. He flipped through the paperwork, then sat back and glanced back up at Reynolds. "You've got a set of balls on you, Reynolds, I'll give you that."

"W-what is it?" June asked.

"It's a request for dismissal," Reynolds said in that same patient, triumphant voice.

June and Clive glanced at each other, then at their lawyer, completely lost. Norris turned a remarkable shade of crimson. It started at his neck and slowly burned up his face where it settled in the balls of his cheeks and the dilated spiderweb of veins on the tip of his nose.

"In English," Clive said.

Norris looked put out. "Essentially, it's paperwork withdrawing your claim for custody."

"Why would we do that?" June said. "We've gone through the evaluations. With flying colors, I might add. We have our court date next week."

"They've got nothing," Norris said. "Their backs are against the wall. They've got nothing to lose by trying a little gamesmanship."

"That's where you're wrong," Reynolds pulled out another document and slid it over to Norris. It was titled the same but was almost twice as thick. "The first would keep the allegations detailed within out of the public record, which I would imagine your clients would prefer. But I would be quite happy to file this second request for dismissal."

As Norris read the new document the crimson drained from his face until he'd turned a sickly shade of white. "This is preposterous." Though the way he said it, the words lacked conviction.

"Not according to the attached affidavits." Reynolds maintained his decorum, and Levi tried to sit back and let it play out, but his heart hammered in his chest so loud, it was almost easier to read lips.

Clive slammed his hand on the table. June jumped. Reynolds smiled.

"I demand to know what's going on," Clive said.

"According to this document, Mae confided in her therapists that she suffered from..." The red returned to Norris' face, and he couldn't quite meet Clive's eyes. "From abuse. Of a sexual nature."

"I don't see what that has to do with our getting custody," Clive blustered.

What surprised Levi the most was the revelation hadn't surprised either Clive or June. Olivia squeezed his hand tighter. He glanced over at her and raised his brow asking if she'd known. Olivia shook her head.

"Because you were the one who abused her, *Dad*."

All heads turned to the doorway where Randy stood in his wrinkled suit with his hair disheveled. To Reynolds, he said, "Sorry, I couldn't stand in the hallway and take it any longer."

"Well, I never," June huffed, seeming more shocked to see who the witness was than by the actual accusation.

"That's right, Mother. You never. You never quit looking the other way. You never told Dad no. You never made him stop. You never took Mae's side over his." Randy's hands shook as he scrubbed them through his hair. "I was a kid back then. I didn't understand what was going on. But I'm an adult now. What you two did was unforgivable. I'm not going to stand by and let the two of you destroy Clementine the way you destroyed Mae."

Reynolds took the first document and slid it down the table to Clive. "I suggest you sign. A decent lawyer would advise you to do the same."

"You have no real proof." Norris finally found his voice. "Just because Mae told her therapists she'd been abused doesn't mean she *was* abused. Or abused by her father. She could have been lying."

Levi couldn't keep silent any more. "Who the hell lies about something like that?"

"We may not have physical proof. Only the subpoenaed testimony of her therapists as well as Randy's testimony."

Mae and Clive glared at Randy who stood his ground, arms crossed.

"But either way, we go to court, this secret comes out." Reynolds' level gaze traveled from June to Clive. "Are you prepared for friends, family, parishioners to hear these accusations about what you did to your own daughter?" His gaze went back to June. "The evil you failed to protect your daughter from?"

June swallowed hard, her eyes staring down at the table. Olivia let out a long-held breath, reminding him to take one of his own before spots appeared in front of his eyes.

"Can I go now?" Randy asked Reynolds.

Reynold nodded. "Yes. Thank you for coming. I know this couldn't have been easy for you."

Clive glared at his son as if the familial betrayal had cut deep. Levi almost laughed at the hypocrisy. What about Clive's ultimate betrayal of his daughter?

"Aunt June," Olivia said, her voice barely a whisper. "Is this true?"

June didn't answer or raise her gaze from the table. Pursing her lips, she reached for the pen and the first document and scribbled her name on the last sheet of paper and handed it to Clive. She reached down, gathered her purse, and left the conference room.

"I could fight this. I'm a deacon. A pillar of the church, of the community—"

"*Clive*," Norris said. "Sign the damn paper."

———

Olivia stood next to her stock trailer at the Caddo Parish fairgrounds near Shreveport, Louisiana. The mid-day sun made sweat break out on her skin, and the rising humidity made the air thick as soup.

"You sure you want to do this? It's not too late to back out," Mr. Cox said.

"I'm positive." Olivia accepted the cash from Cox Ranch, No Bull's chief competition in Texas for roughstock supply. "Jettison is still a great bull, but his questionable infertility won't help my breeding program any." Besides, she had big plans for the money the bull would bring.

Within minutes, she signed over the transfer papers and Rusty helped the Cox Ranch boys load Jettison onto their trailer. When they'd finished, and Cox and his new bull were on their way home, Rusty asked, "You headed back to Texas tonight?"

It was late Sunday night, and the rodeo had ended a few hours before. Rusty and the rest of her crew had a long drive to get to Florida, so they were about to hit the road.

"First thing tomorrow. I've got business to take care of in the morning."

She still hoped she'd made the right decision about tomorrow's purchase. It was the biggest expenditure she'd be making without consulting Levi. Not that No Bull wasn't hers to run, but he was her husband, and they were running it together. Which meant they generally discussed the big sales beforehand. Except, she wasn't sure Levi would approve, and she was hoping for forgiveness in place of permission.

When she got to her motel room, she dialed the operator

and placed a collect call to the ranch. Levi picked up after a single ring.

He was out of breath when he answered. Clementine must be asleep if he was sprinting for the phone. "Hello?"

"It's me."

Levi's deep chuckle sent heat to her core, and she wished she'd been able to complete her business that night, so she could have made it home in time to crawl into bed with him. "Hey, me." Levi's voice shifted down an octave or two. He knew that always got her juices flowing. The damn man never played fair.

"I should be home by early afternoon tomorrow."

"You've got some explaining to do."

That's not the response she'd expected. "What do you mean?"

"What's with the construction equipment that showed up today?"

Ummm... Shit. They weren't supposed to come until later in the week.

"*Liv.*" Levi used his stern voice. The what-have-you-got-up-your-sleeve voice.

"What did gramps tell you?"

"To ask you about it."

Phew. "I promise I'll tell you tomorrow, okay?"

His "okay" came on the heels of a reluctant, indulgent sigh.

She quickly changed the subject because she was so excited about what she had planned she didn't think she could keep from telling him if he pressured her. "That Curry kid asked for your number. Did he get hold of you?"

"Yeah. Get this. He and Jameson are interested in bulldogging coaching."

"I told you if you put the word out, you'd find people interested."

"I guess. I feel like I'm putting the cart before the horse. I don't have the proper facilities for that kind of training."

Don't tell him. Don't tell him. But God, she wanted to. "You gotta start somewhere."

She heard rustling over the phone and Levi's muffled voice said, "Hey, Pix, what are you doing out of bed?" Then he came back on the line and said, "Hey, I gotta go. I think Clementine had a bad dream. Drive safe. I love you."

"Love you, too."

She got a speeding ticket on the way home the next day. Almost got another one ten miles from home. She pulled into the long driveway to her ranch, her windows down, the warm breeze blowing in.

Up ahead she saw the earth-moving equipment, the trucks filled with dirt and sand. At least they hadn't tried to start the work before she'd returned.

As she drove by the house and parked next to the barn, Chunk whinnied in the trailer. Her bucking stock whinnied back.

Levi came out of the barn, Clementine in one hand and the lead rope to a freshly bathed and brushed pony in the other. The pony whinnied. Chunk returned the call.

Olivia came around the front of the truck. Levi's steps faltered as his eyes focused on the trailer. He dropped Clementine's hand and tied the pony to the trailer. Olivia went to her knees and scooped Clementine up when she ran into her arms.

"*Liv.*" Levi's coarse voice proved difficult to hear over Clementine's chattering. He didn't look excited, or pleased, or angry or...*anything.*

Oh, God. Had she royally screwed up?

"What have you done?" Then he did a double take on the trailer. "And where's Jettison?"

It was then that Clementine noticed who was in the trailer. "Chunky!"

Chunk nickered, and Olivia put Clementine down. Clementine ran to the trailer and climbed up on the bumper, sticking her fingers through the slats to scratch Chunk's fuzzy nose.

Olivia stepped over to Levi and wrapped an arm around his waist. Red rimmed his eyes and the sun glinted off the moisture gathering there.

"I don't understand what's going on," he said at last.

"You can't teach bulldogging without a good bulldogging horse."

He glanced down at her. "We don't have the money for—" Levi cut himself off as the realization sank in. "*Jettison.*" It came out as a statement, but it was more of a question.

She nodded.

He waved his hand in the general direction of the construction equipment. "And this?"

"Jettison sold at a very fair price. There was enough money to buy back Chunk and build the arena and chutes you need to run your bulldogging school."

"It's too much. You should have talked to me. It could be years before a school is profitable, if it ever is. I—" He looked dumbfounded. "Why?"

"You made a promise to me to put our family first. You've done that. Each and every day. But putting Clementine, me, and this ranch first doesn't mean sacrificing your dreams as well. I want you to have this. For you. For us."

Clementine hopped off the trailer's running board and ran back to Levi. "Daddy! I wanna ride Chunky!"

Levi laughed. "So do I, Pix. So do I." He picked her up and held her on his hip then wrapped an arm around Olivia's neck and brought her in for a kiss.

"Eew, gross."

Levi chuckled and pulled away. "You shouldn't have done it. But, babe, I'm so glad you did." He squeezed her tight against him again, and she knew that in his arms was where she wanted to be for the rest of her life.

"You know," she said, "you once asked me what I was afraid of. I now know what that was."

"Yeah?"

"I was afraid I couldn't make you happy. Not really. I want this for you. I want you to be as happy as you've made Clementine and me."

He put Clementine down and pulled Olivia in close.

Clementine bopped him on the leg. "*Daddy.*"

"Hang on, Pix." He cupped Olivia's cheek. "You didn't have to do this to make me happy. I love you, Liv. That's what matters."

He kissed her then, to a chorus of Clementine's complaints, pouring himself, his emotions, his soul into her. It made her heart swell. She had a hard time catching her breath. When he finally pulled back, she said, "So does that mean you want me to call the construction off?"

He laughed. "Oh, hell, no."

Chunk stomped in the trailer. Clementine took Levi's hand and started pulling him toward the rear door.

"I'll get him," Olivia said, as she opened the trailer and led Chunk out.

She took Clementine's hand and handed Levi the rope. Chunk took a step forward, planting his head in the middle of Levi's chest. His fingers found the itchy spots on Chunk's chest.

Levi whispered in his horse's ear, loud enough for Olivia to hear, "Looks like we're both home now."

LETTER TO MY READERS

Dear Reader,

A blast from the past is always a kick, but now it's time to return to the present, to a ranch that'll make you want to strap on your spurs.

Running from her past has led battle-scarred veteran Mackenzie Parish into unfamiliar territory—a Wyoming ranch. She's survived enough violence to last a lifetime, but middle America isn't much safer than Iraq.

Not when the ranch becomes a target.

Now lives are in danger.

Can an ex-bull rider's sweet touch draw Mackenzie out of herself—and her painful past?

Or will Mackenzie have to choose between saving herself, and the man who has made her feel whole again?

You'll want to hang onto your hat because *Cowgirl, Unexpectedly* is a sexy, gritty ride you won't want to miss.

Your next adventure starts here: www.books2read.com/CU62

ALSO BY VICKI THARP

Lazy S Ranch Series

Cowgirl, Unexpectedly (Book 1)

Must Love Horses (Book 2)

Hot on the Trail (Book 3)

Cowboy, Undercover (Book 4)

Rockin' Rodeo Series

Luck of the Draw (Book 1)

Photo Chute (Book 2)

Reined In (Book 3)

Wright's Island Series

Don't Look Back (Book 1)

In Her Defense (Book 2)

ABOUT THE AUTHOR

Vicki Tharp makes her home on small acreage in south Texas with her husband and an embarrassing number of pets. When she isn't writing, you can usually find her on the back of her horse—avoiding anything that remotely resembles housework—smelling like fly spray and horse sweat.

Join my newsletter at: http://eepurl.com/croJgz
Join my street team and receive free Advance Reader Copies of my upcoming books at: http://eepurl.com/cWhXbD
You can find my website at: www.VickiTharp.com
I love to hear from readers. You can email me at Author@VickiTharp.com

Or you can stalk me at:

facebook.com/VickiTharpAuthor

instagram.com/author_Vicki_Tharp

bookbub.com/authors/vicki-tharp

amazon.com/author/vicki_tharp

twitter.com/vwtharp

www.ingramcontent.com/pod-product-compliance
Lightning Source LLC
Chambersburg PA
CBHW050522190726
48284CB00003B/910